No female was impervious to Sawyer Buchanon.

Except Jade. Even if he had a kind side, and he did, and even if she found him attractive—and who wouldn't?—he was a Buchanon. And her maiden name was on his father's naughty list.

He spotted her inside the dim room with the baby and raised both palms in a comical, supplicating gesture.

"What's this? You've ditched me for a younger man?"

"His toothless grin was irresistible."

Sawyer paused for one second as if her banter caught him off guard. She knew he considered her humorless and cold, which was for the best, but she wasn't always that way.

Crossing the room, Sawyer swooped Ashton into his arms. "You ready? Where's the squirt's bag?"

She reached for the backpack but Sawyer beat her to it, swung it over his opposite shoulder, and they headed out for the day.

The sight of the man with a baby in his tanned, muscled arms tugged at Jade's insides. He was a puzzle she couldn't fit into her tidy mental box.

Linda Goodnight, a *New York Times* bestselling author and winner of a RITA® Award in inspirational fiction, has appeared on the Christian bestseller lists. Her novels have been translated into more than a dozen languages. Active in orphan ministry, Linda enjoys writing fiction that carries a message of hope in a sometimes dark world. She and her husband live in Oklahoma. Visit her website, lindagoodnight.com, for more information.

Books by Linda Goodnight

Love Inspired

The Buchanons

Cowboy Under the Mistletoe
The Christmas Family
Lone Star Dad
Lone Star Bachelor

Whisper Falls

Rancher's Refuge
Baby in His Arms
Sugarplum Homecoming
The Lawman's Honor

Redemption River

Finding Her Way Home
The Wedding Garden
A Place to Belong
The Christmas Child
The Last Bridge Home

Visit the Author Profile page at Harlequin.com for more titles.

Lone Star Bachelor

Linda Goodnight

Recycling programs
for this product may
not exist in your area.

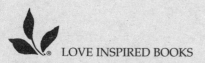 LOVE INSPIRED BOOKS

ISBN-13: 978-0-373-89933-3

Lone Star Bachelor

Copyright © 2017 by Linda Goodnight

www.Harlequin.com

Printed in U.S.A.

Out of the same mouth proceed blessing and cursing. My brethren, these things ought not to be so.
—*James* 3:10

For my forever friend, Trisha Hayes. We've been through a long journey together over many years and many tears, laughter, music and kids. Always, always, I knew I could lean on you for prayer and love and enduring friendship. And the turquoise jewelry ain't bad either! Love you, sweet lady. This one is for you.

Chapter One

It was now or never. Walk up to that door and knock or drive back to the office and give the case to someone else.

From behind the wheel of her plain white Chevy Cruze, Jade Warren eyed the housing complex next to the smooth green golf course of Gabriel's Crossing, Texas. She wasn't a bit surprised that Sawyer Buchanon lived in such a nice place. His family's construction company had likely built the buff brick townhomes, something she would know if she'd done her computer homework. But the impulse to immediately drive to the river town and face the dragon had overshadowed her usual rigid work ethic.

Do the job. Do it right. Don't get involved.

Which was exactly why she shouldn't have accepted this assignment.

She *was* involved. She'd been involved for

years. Being here, accepting this investigation, made her a traitor.

But frankly she was tired of chasing absconding debtors and deadbeat exes. She wanted a case with meat on the bones, something she could sink her investigating teeth into.

Most of all, she was curious about her family nemeses, the dreaded Buchanons.

To hear her daddy tell it, the Buchanons breathed fire and plotted the demise of anyone they didn't like. And they always won. She'd grown up despising a group of people she'd never met.

Until today.

A pretty redhead exited the front door of number 4, Sawyer Buchanon's home. Figures. Very little investigative skill was required to learn Sawyer liked women and they liked him back. His social media was loaded with messages and photos from beautiful females.

The shapely, jean-clad redhead hopped into the cab of a bloodred F-150 pickup complete with a big white toolbox across the back.

Jade waited until the woman pulled away, the truck's mufflers rumbling, before leaving her nondescript car to walk across the lush, manicured grass, up the clean-swept sidewalk past recently groomed boxwood to ring the doorbell.

Before she had time to put on her game face, Sawyer Buchanon, in gray athletic pants and white T-shirt, opened the door.

Jade thought she had prepared for this moment. She'd seen his photos. She knew he was very handsome and was determined not to react, not to become distracted from the case, or worse, become an idiot female and simper.

She swallowed and breathed slowly through her nose in a concerted effort to keep her expression cool and passive.

Photos didn't do the man justice. Messy midlength hair, vivid blue eyes and a morning scruff as black as his hair.

Every female cell in her body reacted. She held the reaction inside, tightening her mouth to a determined thin line.

Sawyer flashed a movie star smile, a little crooked and a lot breathtaking.

Jade clamped her back teeth against her cheek until pain shot from the roof of her mouth to the top of her head.

There. Better. He wasn't *that* good looking.

"Did you forget somethi— Oh, I thought you were Clare." He poked his head around the door and looked toward the driveway. "She just left."

Right. The redhead.

Jade stuck out a hand, her words intentionally crisp. "I'm Jade Warren, Paris Investigations. Is this a good time for us to talk?"

His smile faltered, replaced by a look of bewilderment. "You're the private investigator my father hired?"

"Yes. Is there a problem?" She braced for it.

"Does my dad know you're…?"

Her hackles rose. "A woman?"

"I was going to say pretty." He flashed the smile again, eyes alight with mischief, and stepped to one side. "Come in. I was about to have a Coke. Want one?"

She shook her head. "Too early in the morning."

"That's what I've been told." He led the way into the living room. The interior surprised her somewhat. Given his reputation, she'd expected a bachelor's lair but was met with clean, simple lines in tones of gray and white with splashes of maroon. Masculine. Tasteful. Jade settled on the dove-gray sofa. Directly in front of it was a big-screen television mounted above a small tiled fireplace.

While Sawyer disappeared around a wall for his caffeine, she took out a notebook and jotted a few lines.

He popped back into the room. "I have coffee."

"I'm good, thank you."

He held up a single-serving coffee pod. "K-cups. Only take a minute. Would you rather have hot chocolate? Cider?" He turned the packet up close to his eyes and pretended to squint. "Caramel vanilla cream?"

She loved caramel vanilla cream. So, apparently, did his legion of girlfriends. Probably including the shapely redhead.

With a soft hum, she scribbled *player* on her pad. Now he was showing his true colors. "Do you stock every flavor?"

"Never know when you'll need them." He grinned. "I aim to please."

Jade didn't roll her eyes but she came close. *Give it a rest, Romeo. I know your kind. I even have the scars to prove it.*

"How nice." She didn't smile. "I'd prefer to get down to business if you don't mind."

"Okay." Coke can in hand, he stood in the doorway between the living room and whatever was behind the wall. Kitchen, apparently. "Shoot."

She wished he would sit down. From her place on the couch she had to look up and it made her feel inferior. At a disadvantage. He was a good six feet tall but not particularly broad. Just fit and lean with the right amount of shoulders. Strong and muscular as she'd expect of a man who made his living with a hammer and his hands.

Not that she noticed shoulders. She'd never known any worth leaning on.

Nor did she allow herself to be intimidated. Maintaining a businesslike tone, she held his gaze and absolutely refused to blink first.

"I'm here to investigate the vandalism plaguing Buchanon Built Construction projects. Your father shared some background with my boss and I have the police reports, but I'll need you to fill me in on details from your perspective."

"You'd do better to discuss this with Brady. He's the site manager and COO of Buchanon Built." A pair of eyebrows, as black as sin's underbelly, twitched with a hint of amusement. "But he's in Italy on his honeymoon. Lucky duck."

Jade flipped through her notes. "Brady. Your older brother. A pet project of his burned to the ground on New Year's Eve."

The handsome face darkened. "Arson. Abby's house. He was building it for her as a Christmas makeover."

"Abby. Brady's wife."

"Fiancée at the time of the fire."

She scribbled a note. "Interesting, but your father is more concerned about the photo recently found after a break-in."

Sawyer made a noise deep in his throat. "Dad has it in his head that Dawson or me—Dawson's my twin—is somehow to blame for all this trouble."

"Why would he think that?"

"Beats me. You'd think he'd focus on Brady. After all, Brady's project was torched, not mine, but someone leaves a picture and Dad suddenly points at us. Me in particular."

"Why you over Dawson?"

"The hair. His is different."

"And this was apparent in the photo?"

Sawyer emitted a frustrated breath. "Yep."

"I'll want to see that photo and speak to your brother, of course."

He jacked a thumb to the south. "He lives next door."

"Yes, I know."

He looked discomfited. "Exactly how much do you know about us?"

She curved her lips for the first time, a cat's smile that had nothing to do with humor. "The more I know, the faster I can solve this case."

"Buchanon Built has dealt with a vandalism problem off and on for going on two years." He pushed away from the wall, his body language clearly indicating he doubted her. "Do you seriously think you can discover something the police and fire investigators can't?"

He had no idea how much fuel his doubts added to her determination. "They have other cases. You have my full focus."

The smile appeared again. He was good at that. Flashing those white teeth against Texas-tanned skin with stunning effectiveness. "And you'll have mine."

His entire focus? She doubted that, not with gorgeous redheads coming and going at random. Women crawling out of the woodwork.

She held his gaze and refused to acknowledge the zip of energy caused by staring into eyes that flashed like blue lightning and were every bit as mesmerizing.

Cam was like this, charming and magnetic. And dangerous.

She ducked her head, annoyed at the direction of her thoughts. The ugly business with Cam was eons behind her and that's where it needed to remain.

During her four-year stint as a police officer, before joining Paris Investigations, she'd interviewed plenty of nice-looking men and dozens of creeps. A pretty face and infectious smile did not sway her. Not anymore. Cam had taught her a painful lesson she wasn't likely to forget.

So save your smiles for someone else, Mr. Buchanon. I know your kind.

"Do you have anything to hide? Anything you'd rather the rest of the world didn't know?"

He blinked, startled by the vehemence of the question. Good. She'd knocked the grin off his face.

After sipping at his soda in contemplation, he ambled across the living room and sank onto a chair across from her. Lanky, agile and oozing manly appeal.

"Are we exchanging secrets?"

She cocked an eyebrow at him, keeping her stare as cool as November. *Get this straight, buster. I know the ploys of a handsome man and I will never, ever fall for that again.*

"Okay." He lifted a hand in surrender. "I guess that would be a negative. In which case, my answer is no. No secrets. No skeletons. Except for a couple of speeding tickets and maybe that one other time."

She sat up straighter. "What other time?"

He chuckled and pointed his Coke, clearly trying to rile her. "Got you interested, didn't I?"

Jade's insides did a slow burn. Mr. Playboy refused to take her seriously.

"Mr. Buchanon, this is a legal investigation, not a contest, and certainly not a joking matter. Do you, or do you not, want to find out who is sabotaging your building projects?"

He sobered. "Sorry. It's just that the whole idea of hiring a PI is ludicrous. A waste of money."

A red flag rose. Did he indeed have something to hide? Some reason he didn't want her to discover? "You object to the investigation?"

"I object to wasting time and money."

Maybe. But Buchanons had plenty. Maybe the money comment was a smoke screen. "Will I have your cooperation?"

"You will, but I don't know anything that's not in the police reports."

Her lips curved again in a humorless smile.

"Let me be the judge of that."

Sawyer squinted at the woman sitting on his couch and rubbed a hand over the discombobulated feeling in his chest while mulling the previous ten minutes.

Jade Warren, for some reason, had decided not to like him, and he tried to understand why. When he'd seemed surprised at seeing her standing on his itty-bitty porch, she'd jumped to immediate conclusions and practically accused him of misogyny.

He bit back a grin. Sawyer Buchanon was anything but a woman hater.

Granted, he'd been surprised at the investigator's gender considering her profession, but he certainly didn't object. Just as he didn't object to women in the construction business.

Take Clare Hammond, for instance. A great trim carpenter, she beat him to the job every morning. Like today, while he'd still been slouching around the town house, Clare had dropped by to return a set of miter clamps he'd inadvertently left behind. She'd been on the job since six. What a work ethic! And she was easy on the eyes, too.

Sawyer also knew Clare took flack at times for being a woman in what was traditionally a man's world, and being pretty was not to her advantage on a construction crew. She had to work hard to prove she was as good at her job as the men. Even then, some crews frowned on having a female on the job site.

But not Buchanon Built Construction Company. When Dad said equal-opportunity employer, he meant it. If a woman could do the job, do it well in a timely fashion and take the inevitable joking that happened on every crew, she was hired. Dad was no dummy. All he had to do was look around at his own family. The Buchanon women were as strong and independent as they came, and Sawyer respected those traits, just as he respected all women.

He also adored them. A woman like Clare who could work him into the ground fascinated him. Women were, in his view, the most blessed gender. They made the world a happier, prettier, kinder place.

So if he had to hang out with someone prying into his life, he'd rather have the vulnerable-looking blonde with the bee-stung mouth than some trench-coat-wearing, smoke-scented gumshoe with an attitude.

Not that Miss Jade Warren didn't have an attitude. She did. A very cold attitude that said she suspected him of something heinous, like sinking the Titanic single-handedly.

She sat on the edge of his sofa, as straight and stiff as a planed two-by-four, hand poised over a notebook. Not a cell phone as he would have used for notes. An old-fashioned notebook.

Except for the clipped tone and suspicious gray eyes that seemed to take in every element in his living room, Little Miss Magnum PI looked too soft and small to investigate anything. Maybe that was her strategy to fool the guilty.

If Sawyer was guilty of anything, she'd have

had him in handcuffs by now. Her long eyelashes, mysterious and dark against pale cheeks, captivated his attention.

She flicked a glance up at him. His breath stuttered and a moth took flight in his midsection.

Whoa. Weird. Nice weird but still weird. He liked women but he could normally maintain coherent thought in their presence.

Jade Warren was different.

There was no good reason in the world for him to be attracted to her. She was too cold, too tight-lipped, too suspicious. But interest bubbled up anyway.

A mouth like hers was made to smile, and he wondered what it would take to make her laugh.

Not that he saw that happening in the next five minutes. Talk about chilly—and yet somebody needed to remind the woman of the outside temperature. Texas in summer scorched, but here she was in a nifty black business suit, tucked in and buttoned up as if she dared anyone to notice she was female.

Sorry to burst your bubble, lady. Even in long pants and sensible shoes—also black—you are all woman. Above the white button-down blouse was a pair of fascinating gray eyes. The color of his couch. Smoke and mystery.

Sawyer took a stinging gulp of Coke, letting the burn brand some sense into him. At the Huckleberry Addition, he had a massive built-in china hutch waiting for his hammer and expertise. He couldn't sit here and contemplate the novelty of a female private investigator who'd managed to both insult and interest him. Maybe more than interest him.

He glanced at his watch. "Ask me whatever you need to. But talk fast. I have to meet my brother at the building supply center in thirty minutes."

"We have a lot to discuss. I need more time with you than that."

He tilted his head. "Time's an important commodity for me, too."

"When can we meet again?"

Sawyer couldn't help himself. He grinned. "Are you asking me out?"

She glared icicles at him. The temperature in the room fell ten degrees. No wonder she wore a black suit. The chill emanating from her could cause frostbite.

Sawyer rubbed his bare arms and fought back a grimace. Prickly little woman, this PI. Pretty and prickly.

"Mr. Buchanon—"

"Sawyer." He held up a hand. "Before you pounce, I apologize. Joking around is my style."

"Not mine."

Sawyer bit back a sigh.

Well, wasn't she more fun than a dental drill? Maybe Dad should have hired a smoke-scented gumshoe after all.

Chapter Two

The Gabriel's Crossing Building and Supply Company spanned a full block and was one of Sawyer's favorite places to shop, if you called buying boards and nails shopping.

Employees knew him by name and catered to his needs as a trim carpenter specializing in beautiful cabinetry and other built-ins. To top it all off, the coffee and popcorn were free.

He stood next to the fragrant machines, munching hot, salty corn while waiting for Dawson. His twin had hit the neighborhood pool early this morning while Sawyer ran five miles around the golf course, their usual routine. Sawyer ran. Dawson swam. He'd not bothered to inform the know-it-all investigator of this fact. That she hadn't headed over to Dawson's condo was a good sign that she already knew their daily routines, an unsettling thought. Though he had nothing to hide, he wasn't wild about the idea of someone knowing his every move. Invasive. Like Big Brother or something.

"Sawyer, good morning. May I help you?"

A dark-haired woman in glasses wearing a red apron and carrying a tape measure approached. She'd worked here in the Building and Supply a long time but he could never remember her name. "I'm good. Thanks."

She paused in front of him as if she had something important to say. "I guess you're waiting for Dawson."

"Yep. As usual, I'm here and he's late."

"You're always so punctual. Can I get you anything while you wait? Popcorn or maybe a coffee?" When he hoisted his popcorn bag, she continued, "We have some new router bits you might want to see."

"Thanks, but no. I like to create my own custom designs."

Her smile faltered. "Oh."

She seemed disappointed and he didn't like to hurt anyone's feelings. "On second thought, if those router bits are handy, I'll have a look. Okay?"

The clerk perked right up. She smiled and pushed at her glasses. "I'll grab the examples for you. We have some pretty ones I'd love to have in my new home. When I get married, I mean." Her cheeks reddened.

He glanced at her name tag. Nora. "Are congratulations in order? You getting married soon?"

"Oh. Well. I hope so." She blushed a deeper crimson and flapped a hand in front of her face. "I'll get those samples."

"Thanks, Nora."

Still blushing and smiling, she hurried off.

Mouth dry from the popcorn, Sawyer poured himself a cup of coffee. He wasn't a big coffee man, but the other Buchanons lived on the stuff. Cut a Buchanon and he bled sawdust, coffee and family loyalty.

He stirred too much cream into the foam cup and heard his brother say, "Why not have a glass of milk?"

"Hey." He left the coffee sitting and turned to Dawson, whose black hair was still wet and shiny from his swim. He was a good-looking dude, even if Sawyer did say so. The same height, with the same face, he and his brother were best friends, though their personalities were different.

Dawson was a calm, introspective guy who counseled family and friends with a gentle God-directed wisdom. Dawson was, in a word, sensitive, and noticed nuances and undercurrents in relationships that Sawyer invariably missed.

Sawyer was— Well, he was different. He'd rather make people smile.

"I had a visitor this morning."

"Yeah? Who?" Dawson confiscated the abandoned coffee cup and sipped.

"Private investigator."

The unflappable brother gave a facial shrug. "Dad warned us."

"He didn't warn us about one thing."

An eyebrow shot up. "Yeah? What's that?"

"She's a woman. A young, beautiful woman. Maybe thirty. About this tall." Sawyer indicated shoulder height. "Wavy blond hair to her shoulders. Kind of soft and vulnerable looking. Not your stereotypical PI."

Dawson saluted him with the cup. "You sure noticed a lot about her. You must be interested."

He was, and he couldn't figure out why. "You need to meet her before you form an opinion. Tough lady."

"Hard-boiled?"

"Cold as a grape Popsicle in January."

"Aw, poor Sawyer." Dawson pulled a silly face. "The lady wasn't charmed."

"Not one bit."

Dawson chuckled and toasted him with the cup. "Losing your touch, bro."

The salesclerk—Nora—came around an end cap struggling to juggle several blister-wrapped packages with four wooden cabinet doors. Sawyer leaped forward to help. "Let me carry those. That's too much for one lady."

"Thank you." She beamed up at him as he stood

close enough to take charge of the wooden doors. "These are the new router designs. When I saw them, I thought of you."

Sawyer sorted through the stack, sharing each one with his twin. "Nice. What do you think, Dawson? Can we use some of these?"

Dawson put his finger on one. "This would look great in the Carter house in the Huckleberry Addition."

Nora, standing between the brothers, frowned up at Sawyer. "The Carter house? Is that a new one? I don't remember seeing any invoices with that name."

"It was a spec home until Charity sold it a couple of days ago. Now that we know the owner, we'll be coordinating on the final details with the Carters." Sawyer tapped the router design. "I agree with Dawson. This one's great, but maybe we could take samples of all of them for showing? You never know a buyer's taste."

"Sure!" she said. "We can do that. I'll go in the back and have the guys run some scrap boards for you to take along."

Dawson reached in his pocket and removed two master keys. "Almost forgot. Can you make a couple of copies from these?"

Her smile broadened. "Be glad to. Should I mark them so you'll know them apart?"

"Good idea." He indicated the project name for each key. "Thanks, Nora."

"Anytime." She started off but turned back, gaze falling on Sawyer. "If you need anything else, let me know."

She left them, and the brothers got down to business, going over their respective phone lists of supplies they needed for today's work.

"I think you have another admirer," Dawson said as they walked through the supply building.

"Who?" The private investigator flashed into Sawyer's head. Jade—pretty name, but hard as the jewel she was named for.

"Nora, dimwit. You need an update on your navigation system?"

"The clerk? Nah, she's a great employee. She helps everyone like that."

Dawson tossed the empty cup into a trash can. "She's never brought me samples to look at. Except that time she thought I was you."

"Nothing unusual about that." They were mirror twins. Dawson was right-handed and Sawyer a leftie. Each had an identical birthmark but on opposite shoulders. But many people still confused them because they were otherwise identical. They'd dealt with the twin confusion all their lives and had used it to their advantage many times, particularly during the ornery middle school years.

"Except she called me Sawyer and sort of gushed, getting all red like she did a minute ago." Dawson pitter-pattered a hand over his heart.

"Give it a rest. After being grilled by the private investigator this morning, I'm not thinking about women." None except the PI.

"That bad, huh?"

"You'll get your turn. What I can't figure out is why the focus is on me."

"The photo was you."

True. No matter how he combed his hair, the part fell naturally to the left. Dawson's on the right. Otherwise, they'd never have figured out an identity. Weird that he didn't recall when or where the photo was taken.

"Just because a picture of me was found on a vandalized site doesn't make the discovery significant. Maybe the photo has nothing at all to do with the case."

"Convince Dad of that."

"Right," Sawyer said. "Dad and one female Sherlock Holmes."

The Red River Roost, a long, old-fashioned strip motel complete with a rooster perched in crowing posture above the flashing vacancy sign, looked a little tired but offered extended stays for a price that fit Jade's expense budget. Dale Trentworth, owner of Paris Investigations, squeezed every penny and expected his employees to do the same.

Jade knew all about pinching pennies, and the River Roost, as the manager called the place, wasn't too bad. Located in a residential area on the far side of Gabriel's Crossing, the place should be quiet and restful, and that was all she required.

She pulled her Chevy into the spot in front of Unit Three and got out, peeling off her jacket as she approached her room. To say she was sweltering in this black suit would be a gross understatement. She was a cooked goose, a roasted duck, a rabbit on a spit baking in the Texas sun. Sweaty and sticky, though the day was young, she tossed the jacket over her elbow.

She knew better than to wear black this time of year, but she'd wanted to appear professional and in control. If she'd arrived at Sawyer Buchanon's house in a dress and spiky heels, he might have turned on the charm and distracted her from her questions. Not that he hadn't tried anyway. The man was a born flirt.

She had not been moved. Not one bit.

Well, perhaps a little, but she'd handled him and his charisma. Even if the picture of his too-handsome face kept flashing behind her eyes, she was proud of her cool, competent reaction.

Now that she'd established her professionalism and complete lack of interest in Mr. Playboy Buchanon, the black had to go.

A glance at her cell phone indicated plenty of time to change before her next appointment.

What she wouldn't give to slip into comfortable jeans and a cool tank top, but first impressions mattered in this business. To be taken seriously, she had to work harder than a man. A glance in the mirror wasn't required to remind her of how she looked. Petite. Fragile. An easy mark.

She was neither fragile nor easy, not anymore. But her size wasn't likely to change, and unless she succumbed to plastic surgery. Neither was her baby-doll face.

Well, she was no baby doll. Sawyer Buchanon and his kind better understand that from the get-go.

She was tough and determined.

Fishing for her key, she glanced around, taking mental snapshots of her surroundings. Police work had taught her to be always on the alert, though Gabriel's Crossing, Texas, was about as calm and peaceful a place as she could think of.

Yet someone had sabotaged the Buchanons' work projects. Bad things happened in small towns, only on a lesser scale.

The small motel was sparsely populated this weekday morning. Beneath the awning in front of the office sat a battered green pickup truck with a riding lawn mower in the bed. From somewhere nearby, she smelled the clean, fresh aroma of cut grass.

A gray late-model Hyundai was parked in front of Unit Eight and a cleaning cart sat outside Unit Seven. Out on the street, a black SUV motored slowly past, tires hissing against the hot pavement.

A few doors up at Unit One, a young strawberry blonde exited her room, a chubby-cheeked baby on her hip. Her gaze caught Jade's. She looked worried, her bottom lip caught between her teeth, brow furrowed beneath wispy bangs. She also looked like a kid, sixteen, seventeen at the most.

Watchful but concerned, too, Jade offered a smile. "Cute baby."

Babies got to her in a big way. She'd wanted two or three. Cam hadn't wanted any. He'd made that painfully clear.

The teenager shifted the baby on her hip. "Thanks. Say hi, Ashton."

She lifted the baby's little hand and waved. Jade waved back, and the friendliness must have been the encouragement the girl needed. She glanced toward the parking lot, squared her shoulders and walked the few feet to Jade's door.

Glad she hadn't unlocked her unit, Jade took the girl's measure. She was an inch or two taller than Jade and too thin, her pale skin devoid of makeup. Dressed in jean shorts and a pink T-shirt, she wore cheap flip-flops and had a pink Cupid's heart tattooed on top of her left foot. No other obvious identifying marks.

Jade relaxed. The girl presented no threat that she could detect. She was just a friendly, nervous teenager with a baby wearing only a disposable diaper.

"I was wondering." The girl darted a worried glance at Jade but quickly looked down at her shoes. "I need a ride. Ashton's out of diapers and..." She let the words trail away.

"You don't have a car?"

The red-blond ponytail swished from side to side. "No."

A dozen questions flashed through Jade's mind. Where was this girl's family? What was she doing in a motel? Was she alone?

She caught on the last one. "Are you staying here by yourself?"

"Me and Ashton." The girl focused on the baby and then on Jade. She licked her lips and swallowed.

Nervous. Embarrassed.

Jade logged every movement, assessing. As a cop, she'd dealt with plenty of runaways. Was this another?

"Where do you live?"

The girl shrugged, but her face flushed crimson. "We got kicked out and moved here."

"Kicked out of where?" Jade was being nosy but this girl had asked for a ride. No harm in requesting information in exchange.

"My mom's place. She let me stay for a while after I had Ashton, but—well, money's tight and she has her own problems. She said it was time for us to take care of ourselves."

Nice family. "You have no one else? What about the baby's father?"

The girl rolled her eyes and made a rueful sound. "He skipped out a looong time ago."

The baby started to fuss and squirm in his mother's arms. Sweat beaded on his upper lip. Instinctively, Jade reached out and grasped the little guy's thrashing arm and wiggled it.

"Are you too hot, precious?" she crooned. "You sure are a handsome boy."

The baby quieted instantly, his big brown eyes latched onto her face.

"I think he likes you," the girl said hopefully.

Jade laughed, itching to hold him as she made a quick decision. Walking half a mile to the nearest store for diapers would be miserable for both mom and baby.

"What's your name?"

"Bailey."

"Okay, Bailey. I'm Jade. I need to change clothes but I won't be long. Fifteen minutes or so, maybe. Take the baby back to your room and stay cool. I'll knock on the door when I'm ready and I'll drive you down to the Dollar Store."

Relief washed over the girl like a sudden summer rain. "Thank you so much. I can't pay you but—"

Jade waved her off. The girl probably didn't have two extra nickels. "I'm glad to do it. Ashton is adorable."

And you break my heart.

The key caught and Jade entered the small

motel room, grateful for the blast of cool air chugging from the wall unit.

The room was clean, but that was about all she could say for it. Bed, TV, desk and cheap chair with a tiny bathroom. "All the comforts of home."

She didn't plan to be here long. The Red River Roost would do until she finished the investigation and returned to her nice apartment in Paris, Texas.

Resisting the urge to jump in the shower and cool off, she changed tops and jackets, opting for a white blazer and orchid button-down. Still professional, but definitely cooler.

From beneath the mattress, she withdrew her tiny laptop and booted up, taking a moment to check her email and run through some records sent by her boss, though nothing appeared pertinent to the Buchanon case. At least not yet.

As an afterthought, she pulled up Sawyer's Facebook profile. Social media was an amazing source of information to private investigators and police officers.

She scanned through the recent posts, pausing at one with a puzzled frown. Sawyer had responded to a message with:

Praying for you, man. Hang in there.

In another, he'd posted a scripture.

No one had mentioned his religious affiliation, but Jade had experience with men who wielded scriptures like a weapon. Her father was one of them, battering her, her brothers and mother over the head with the Bible whenever the words suited his intent.

Granted, Sawyer's scripture had been encouraging, not scathing, but religious fanatics were always suspect in her book. Closing the lid, Jade slid the laptop back into its hiding place. She exited the room, still pondering the complexities of human beings, one in particular. She wondered if Sawyer's twin would prove as interesting.

Chapter Three

Buchanon Built Construction Company was housed in a warehouse on the edge of Gabriel's Crossing, not far from the railroad tracks and the downtown area. Every day at least four times, a train rumbled through town, shook the earth, rattled windows and made dogs howl. Townsfolk like Sawyer barely noticed unless they were stuck at the railroad crossing. Like this morning.

When Sawyer finally arrived at the warehouse with Dawson pulling in behind him, a row of familiar pickup trucks had parked at an angle in front. UPS and a flatbed lumber truck unloaded supplies through the end double doors, the clatter of their labor enlivening the quiet, sunny morning. Summer in Gabriel's Crossing meant construction work and plenty of it. Business for the Buchanon family was not good. Business was great.

Sawyer entered through the front door, stepping into the main offices where a U-shaped desk filled most of the room. Two of his sisters were behind the business center, already busy, and the ever-present scents of coffee and new wood welcomed him in.

"Did you bring doughnuts?" Allison asked. His petite sister could normally eat anything without gaining weight, but lately she'd put on a few pounds, mostly around the middle. She was hungry all the time.

"You'd be better off eating something healthy, Allison." Jaylee, stick thin, was super health conscious and happily nagged the rest of them on a regular basis about their food choices. They mostly ignored her.

"I am eating healthy." Allison patted her barely rounded belly. If he hadn't been reminded a hundred times, Sawyer wouldn't even know she was pregnant. "But baby Hamilton wants a doughnut with his milk this morning."

Sawyer held up a white box. "Uncle Sawyer to the rescue."

Allison sucked in a deep, appreciative breath. "My hero."

"I thought Jake was your hero."

"He is, but he's not here and you have doughnuts." She laughed, tossing her flippy dark hair.

"Did the poor guy already have enough of your pregnancy hormones and run away?" He knew better. Jake Hamilton was so thrilled over the expected baby he behaved as if he was the only man ever to experience fatherhood. Not that Sawyer would know a thing about that. Someday he'd like a passel of kids. It was the Buchanon way. But for now, he'd play the happy uncle and teasing brother.

"He and Manny are hauling bulls to the sale." Allison pumped her arm once. "Cha-ching. Gotta buy baby some pretties."

She reached for the doughnut box on the counter and flipped the lid open with an approving moan. "These are amazing. Which do you think is healthiest? The Bavarian cream? Does that count as dairy?"

Jaylee snorted. "If you're going to eat one, pick the one you like best. *Healthy* and *doughnuts* are incompatible terms."

Sawyer reached across the counter and took a chocolate-iced pastry. "Coke, popcorn and doughnuts. My breakfast of champions."

Jaylee swatted at him with a stack of paper. He laughed and added, "I promise to eat a salad for lunch. Anything I need to know before I head on over to the job site?"

"Dad's in the back. He wants to talk before you leave."

Beyond the office space was a conference area for family and vendor meetings and anything else that required a gathering place. Quinn, the family architect, worked there for peace and quiet and because he'd been a reclusive grump since moving home from Dallas a couple of years ago. However, since falling in love with Gena Satterfield, the local nurse practitioner, Quinn was a lot easier to be around.

"Sure thing." Sawyer sauntered through the doorway, mouth full of fried dough. Dawson followed.

When he saw the woman standing stiff as the Statue of Liberty at the end of a long table, he nearly choked.

The fiery attraction he'd hoped was a fluke seared up the back of his neck.

His father, standing next to her, waved them in. "Sawyer, I think you've met Jade Warren from the private investigation firm."

Sawyer battled the doughnut and managed to swallow down the thick lump.

The attraction was an entirely different matter. It raced through his bloodstream like molten lava. Nice. And weird.

He liked fun-loving, happy women with sunny dispositions and lots of laughter. Why did he find the serious, unfriendly Jade so compelling?

"Well, if it isn't Nancy Drew." He offered an intentionally flirty smile, hoping to loosen her up a little.

Her icy stare knocked the smile right out of him. She nodded once, a head bob that was both dismissal and acknowledgment.

Did anything rattle Miss Prim and Grim?

"Let's have a seat," Dad was saying as he pulled out a chair for Jade. Sawyer would have done that. Wanted to do it. Instead he seated himself across from her and noticed she'd changed clothes. She was still buttoned to the top in a choke hold that could take out a sumo wrestler, but the light purple color looked good with her eyes.

Yeah. He was noticing way too much about a woman who really didn't want to like him.

He folded his arms on the tabletop and let his gaze linger on her deceptively sweet face while she talked in that crisp, no-nonsense manner that made him straighten his posture.

"Your father is creating a list of disgruntled employees." She flipped open the spiral notebook. "I'd like each of you to do the same for cross-referencing purposes."

Sawyer exchanged looks with Dawson and they both laughed. They still had the twin radar at times, knowing what the other thought. "Disgruntled? Would that include us brothers? We *stay* disgruntled."

"But Dad won't let us stop working." Dawson lifted his coffee cup in a salute.

Dan Buchanon smiled slightly. "My boys like to joke around."

"I see that." But she didn't crack a smile. "Does anyone come to mind immediately? Anyone who was fired, injured on the job, or caused a problem?

No matter how small or seemingly insignificant the issue, I need to know."

The four men mentioned a handful of people but stalled out quickly. They ran a reputable business and treated employees well. Dan, a workaholic, could be tough and demanding, but Brady, Mom and the three sisters kept things running smoothly so that most employees loved to work for the Buchanons.

Everyone wanted to come to the Buchanon Built Christmas party and the Fourth of July cookout, the place where Dan handed out bonuses and gifts and goodies to show appreciation for the previous six months of success.

"This business goes back many years to Grandpa. Maybe our bad guy goes that far back, too." Dawson's usually serene face was troubled. "I'll give the list more thought."

Sawyer nodded. "Sure. I will, too."

"Have we provided enough to get started?" Dan pushed up from the table. He really was a workaholic. Sitting around for too long made him antsy.

Jade stood as well and tapped a pen against her notebook. "I want to see the vandalized sites today if possible."

"No problem." Dad aimed a finger toward Sawyer. "Sawyer will show you around. You can use the time to discuss anything in his past that may have set someone off on a vendetta."

"Dad! Come on. I'm not the guilty party here. And I have important work to do."

Dan held up a hand, his universal signal for "don't argue."

"Dawson can handle your load today." To Dawson, he said, "Call Clare Hammond to help out in Sawyer's place."

"Works for me." Dawson knocked back the last of his coffee and pushed to a stand. "Clare's a pro, almost as good as us."

Sawyer liked working with her, too. He could actually make Clare laugh, something he couldn't say for the PI. But maybe if he and Jade Warren spent some time together, if she got to know him better, she might loosen up. Maybe he'd even convince her that he was a good guy—a long shot, he thought with humor, but he was always up for a challenge.

And when had he ever refused a day off with a beautiful woman?

Jade's sensible shoes crunched on the gravel parking area outside the Buchanon offices as she made her way to her practical white Chevy. Even after driving her motel neighbor to the store and back, she'd arrived with plenty of time to spare for the meeting with the Buchanon boss. Now that she'd met the main man in person Jade felt better, more in control.

She wished her feelings were the same about

Bailey Shaffer. The kid with the cute baby boy was barely seventeen and completely alone. No education, no job, no transportation. If not for public assistance, she and baby Ashton would have nothing. Bailey seemed like a sweet girl, and her love for Ashton showed on her face and in every action. She was a good, if too young, mother in a very bad situation.

Jade shook her head, knowing she should be focused on the job instead of the teenage mother. But she hurt for the girl and worried about her and the baby.

Sawyer Buchanon was behind her a few paces, having stopped to grab a doughnut from his sisters. He'd offered her one but she'd refused. She didn't know why. She loved doughnuts, especially the ones with chocolate icing and lots of sprinkles, but she didn't want Sawyer to think he could beguile his way under her skin.

Again, she couldn't put a finger on what it was about him. He ruffled her and she didn't like the feeling. It felt like attraction and that scared her. She had always been a sucker for handsome, smiling men until Cam Warren taught her a lesson she couldn't forget. She knew her weaknesses, so she had to be careful. She would not be a victim again.

"Hey, Jade. Hold up."

She stopped, one hand on her car door, keys ready. Sawyer ambled in her direction, the sun glinting on his black hair. He was built tall, like his brothers and father, lean, well-proportioned and fit, with long legs that ate up the ground in no time. She observed him as she would a suspect, wondering what kind of man lived inside that too-perfect body.

Her stomach clenched. Or was that flutters? Awareness flutters.

Annoyed to think it might be, she bit out a reply. "What?"

"Ride with me." He hitched his head. "My truck's over here."

"No need. I'll follow you in my vehicle."

His nostrils flared. He gave her a long, slow look that seared the ends of her hair. "Suit yourself."

Sawyer spun toward his big maroon pickup while Jade contemplated what she'd done. If she wanted to dig into the guy's past, she needed to spend time with him in his environment, get to know more about him than what was on his Facebook page.

Her refusal was a bad sign that he was causing her to react like a woman instead of an investigator. That simply would not do.

"On second thought, I might as well conserve fuel and ride with you." *Nice save, Jade.* And Dale would appreciate her sacrifice.

Sawyer spun back, boots grinding the gravel. He still didn't look happy, but Jade was certain she saw a triumphant gleam in his disturbingly attractive eyes.

Saying nothing, she grabbed her mini back-pack containing camera, notebook, phone and wallet, and followed him to his truck. He opened the door, took her backpack and tossed it into the back of the double cab, and was about to help her up into the high passenger seat. She stared at his outstretched hand.

"I can do it."

His hand didn't budge.

She flashed a quick glance at his face. *Mistake.* Though he neither smiled nor spoke, he stood watching her, serene and easy, as if he helped women into his truck all the time. Which he prob-ably did.

Ignoring him, if such a thing was possible, as well as his offered hand Jade grabbed the side of the door and started to boost herself up. She was woefully short.

Strong, masculine fingers steadied her elbow with exactly the right amount of pressure. Gentle. Steady. Dependable.

Pulse clattering, which annoyed her no end, Jade managed a terse "Thank you."

"No problem. It's the Buchanon way."

Whatever that meant.

These high cabs were a pain, but she was per-fectly capable of helping herself. However, being treated with courtesy and respect was not a bad thing. She wanted that. Courtesy. Respect. But not the warm fuzzies Sawyer seemed to generate in her nerve endings.

As she settled into the oversize vehicle, Sawyer slammed the door, jogged around the front and hopped inside.

"Nice truck." Might as well start with his vehicle, always a good way to get a man talking about himself.

"I like it." He started the engine. A diesel rumble bubbled around them. "You want music?"

"I'm good. Whatever you usually do. Don't let me get in the way." *Let me observe you in your natural habitat, like a lion or a grizzly.*

He flipped on the radio, and contemporary Christian music came through the speakers. He turned the volume to low. "You can change channels if you want."

She said nothing, but made a point to notice everything about the vehicle, jotting notes in her spiral book. The interior smelled like him—woodsy and male—and except for a pair of brown leather work gloves in the seat between them it was devoid of clutter. Unusual for a work vehicle.

She craned her head toward the truck bed. "Where are your tools?"

He kept his eyes on the road. "We pull a trailer onto the job site."

Somewhere between his house and now he'd lost his jaunty attitude and gift of gab. He was none too happy with her, and she was fine with that. He was, however, surprisingly polite about it.

They rode along in silence for a couple more minutes, through pleasant neighborhoods and into the heart of Gabriel's Crossing. The pretty little Texas town had been built near the Red River and, judging by the attention to curb appeal, probably belonged to one of those Main Street America organizations.

Large pots of geraniums and pansies decorated each corner with splashes of color, and brightly painted storefronts were well tended to show off everything from the latest boots and jeans to lawn mowers and lava lamps. A very good artist had painted a pioneer mural down the outside walls depicting a ferry crossing the river while men on horseback and families in wagons waited their turns.

"I don't know what good this will do."

She turned her attention toward him. Even though he stared straight ahead at the street, Jade's stomach did that ridiculously annoying flutter thing. "Excuse me?"

"Visiting the damaged houses." He flicked a glance her way and then looked back at the road. Long, strong fingers lightly sprinkled with dark hair curled around the steering wheel at eight and two. Manly hands devoid of jewelry. A carpenter's hands. "All of them are repaired now and Abby's home is rebuilt. She and Brady put it up for sale."

Since their earlier meeting he'd shaved, a shame from a purely aesthetic perspective, but his smooth profile remained square-jawed perfection. A man ought not to look that good.

She swallowed and watched the passing town instead of Sawyer Buchanon, though her thoughts remained on him. Purely for professional reasons. He was her job.

"It's a new home. Why don't they live there?" she asked.

"Brady already had his own place out in the country when he and Abby realized they couldn't live without each other. They'll live in his house when they get back from Italy." He flipped on the signal light and slowed to turn. "You should see that place. It's spectacular. All kinds of golden wood and native rock. The house is huge, but then, so's my brother."

"I've heard that. He played football at Tech. Linebacker." She wasn't that much of a football fan but no one lived in Texas without being aware of the game.

Sawyer's gaze swung toward her, flashing lightning. He spoke easily but with a bite. "I've no doubt you know where all of us went to college, with info right down to our GPAs."

As a matter of fact, she did. She did not, however, think he would appreciate that information and since she wanted him to talk, she skipped right on past the comment.

"The police ruled out one suspect, Jake Hamilton. He's now your brother-in-law."

"Yeah. Pointing fingers at Jake was a mistake. He's all right. He treats my sister like a princess, and that's good enough for me."

"Then why did you suspect him as the vandal?"

He glanced over, eyebrow jacked. "Don't you already know this information?"

She flipped a page in her notebook. "I want to hear the story from your perspective."

With a button push, he silenced the radio. "Okay, then. In a nutshell. A hunting accident. Jake and Quinn were stupid kids, Quinn in college making a big splash as a pro-bound quarterback."

She knew all that, too, but let him talk. Everybody in Texas and most of America knew about the superstar football player. He'd been in the news, ESPN, *Sports Illustrated* and attended charity benefits constantly until the accident.

"He was up for the Heisman Trophy his freshman year."

"Sophomore, too. Quinn was the man with the golden arm and the big future until he and Jake decided beer and guns were a good mix. Mistaking him for a deer, Jake accidently shot Quinn."

Jade watched his profile, saw the tightening of his mouth and the way his Adam's apple bobbed. He still ached for his brother.

"Destroying his golden arm."

"Right. Quinn's had years of surgeries, rehab,

physical therapy. He'll never be the same, but he's doing okay."

"I can see where that would generate some animosity, but why blame Jake for the vandalism?"

"My brothers weren't exactly excited when Jake and Allison reconnected and fell in love. I think maybe Quinn and Brady were looking for a reason to blame Jake."

"Payback?"

"I suppose, but payback's not usually the Buchanon way." He lifted a finger and motioned toward a housing complex. "There's the Huckleberry Addition up ahead."

"Most of the vandalism has occurred here?"

"All except the time at Abby's house."

"Hmm." She scribbled in her book. "Her place was an anomaly, which may indicate a personal connection in that instance."

"Yes. Maybe. But if that's true, why are all the other crimes here in the Huckleberry Addition? We have other projects going on all the time. And why isn't Brady the focus of your investigation, considering the property was his makeover and the owner was his fiancée?" He pulled alongside a curb and stopped the truck.

"Fair question. My focus is on all areas, not you only." Definitely not. Not with the way her blood pressure spiked every time he beamed those electric eyes in her direction.

"Brady will get his share of attention when

he returns from that honeymoon." She slid the backpack over her shoulder. "Unless I've already solved the case."

"I hope you can."

So did she. "Can we talk a minute before I see the homes?"

He paused, one hand on the door lever. "What about?"

"You."

His head dropped back and he groaned. "Dad won't be satisfied until you do, so go ahead. I have all day."

"Does that bother you?"

He hiked an eyebrow. "Does what bother me?"

"Spending the day with me."

Sawyer studied her for several uncomfortable seconds, his expression serious. She expected some flirtatious remark, a come-on.

Instead, he said, "The jury is still out on that."

"Fair enough." She was disappointed and the reaction ruffled her. Why should she care one way or the other whether he enjoyed her company? He was a client, not a friend. "I'll need a list of all your friends, particularly women you've dated recently, along with their contact information."

"That's a bit invasive, isn't it?"

"Part of the investigation. Jilted girlfriends can sometimes harbor anger for a long time. You know the old adage. There is no fury like a woman scorned."

"Scorned?" He frowned and his eyebrows dipped as if she'd insulted him. "I'm not that kind of guy."

She'd be the judge of that. "Are you seeing anyone now?"

"Not anyone special, if that's what you mean. Are you?"

His tone was relaxed and conversational but Jade stiffened anyway. Her traitorous pulse jumped higher than a kangaroo on a trampoline.

With self-protecting snarkiness, she crossed her arms tightly and glared. "I'm asking the questions, if you don't mind. Who have you dated in the last month?"

Sawyer shifted in his bucket seat, bounced a fist against the steering wheel and, with a sigh, reluctantly mentioned two names.

He had to be lying. While assuring herself her interest was purely professional, she pressed. "That's all? Two?"

He gave her a puzzled look. "Clare and I are work pals, though, nothing serious there. We work together sometimes, so occasionally we grab dinner or watch a ball game. She's fun. Knows how to laugh and have a good time."

Was there something pointed in his remark? Did he think she was as dull as used dishwater?

With a sniff and an internal reminder that he was one of the subjects in this investigation, she tapped the other name on the too-short list.

"And Lacy?"

"Great girl. She golfs on the course near my house. We've played a few rounds. Gone out a few times."

The tension returned to her shoulders. "Are you still seeing her?"

"Not lately. Both of us have been too busy." He folded his arms over the steering wheel. "Is this really necessary? The women I know are good people. And I'm not all that. They aren't breaking into houses over me."

"Stranger things have happened."

He made a derisive hiss, like a tire going flat.

She asked a few more questions but Sawyer refused to say much about the women he dated beyond their names, even when she pushed back into his college days. He was popular. She knew that from his social media, but he didn't brag. If he'd had conquests or left a trail of angry broken hearts, he wasn't going to tell her. Jade found that both admirable and frustrating.

"I'm sure I'll have more questions later." She closed her notebook with a businesslike snap. "But for now, let's have a look at those houses."

"The interrogation is over. Big yea."

She hitched an eyebrow at him. "For now."

He exhaled a gusty breath, tilted his head back and looked toward the sky. "Great."

With a pinch of satisfaction at ruffling him, Jade pushed open the heavy door.

Sawyer came around to her side of the pickup but she'd already slid to the pavement, hitting with a jarring thud.

He noticed the abrupt landing but didn't say anything.

Her pride was getting the best of her. She should have waited for him. It was a long way down in these high-rise pickup trucks. Especially for a small person.

She straightened her blazer and her shoulders, but even with her best posture she struck Sawyer only about halfway up on his blue T-shirt. Right in that muscular bow of pecs and biceps.

"This was the first house hit," he said, "about a year and a half ago."

Jerking her attention to the house, Jade lifted her camera and snapped photos. The home he indicated, now occupied, was a beautiful modern brick with a double garage and bright red front door.

The other homes around the neighborhood were similar in style but unique enough to avoid the cookie-cutter look of some housing developments. Different colors or shutters, a few different designs. And the landscaping was the perfect blend of trees, small shrubs and smooth grass.

"The police report said the damage at this address was all cosmetic." She snapped more photos.

"Mostly paint and graffiti."

"Damage escalated with each attack. That has to be significant."

"I never gave it much thought, but I guess it did."

"One of the first things I looked at when I received the police reports." She'd laid them out end to end and created a spreadsheet, chronicling every bit of reported damage. "I graphed the escalation."

He flashed that smile. "Brainy woman. I like it."

She was, and she was also smart enough not to be led astray by a handsome face, blue eyes and a compliment. Even if he affected her blood pressure and didn't kiss and tell.

"Which other houses in this neighborhood were hit?"

"Come on. If you're up for a walk, I'll show you around."

"Of course." As a former cop, she stayed in top shape. A walk, even in the Texas heat, would not deter her.

Leaving the truck parked along the curb, they walked the area, four square blocks of beautiful Buchanon Built homes. Signs heralding their construction company stabbed the ground in front of several yet to be sold.

Sawyer's long legs outpaced her but when he realized she trailed him by several yards, he slowed, adjusting his speed to hers. In his relaxed manner, he chatted about the area, pointing out the attractive features like a real estate salesman.

He was easy in his skin, a confident man.

Across the street, a home owner with a toddler in tow exited one house and waved. Jade's thoughts zoomed to the young mother at the motel. She wasn't in Gabriel's Crossing to baby-sit teenage mothers but it wouldn't hurt to check on the pair after work, to make sure Bailey and Ashton had something to eat.

Sawyer lifted a hand and greeted the home owner by name.

"How are you doing, Maggie? Enjoying your new home?"

"Loving it. You guys do great work." She lifted the toddler into a car seat.

"Thanks. I'll pass along the compliment."

The woman waved again as she drove away.

Friendly. Attractive to women. Was Sawyer truly a nice guy? Or was his smile and friendliness a facade to get what he wanted? Like Cam's?

Troubled at the line of thought and the way she couldn't stop noticing Sawyer as a man, Jade forced her attention back to the houses. Do the job. Do it right. Focus on the investigation.

She asked questions, took photos, made notes and considered the location of this particular housing complex. They'd built on the edge of a rural area but close enough to town for convenience, a perfect location for those wanting expansive lawns and a little privacy without all those board fences. The kind of neighborhood where kids could safely play outside, roller-skate and ride bikes.

She'd love to live in a family-friendly place like this.

"Why this housing addition? Was there a problem with any of the nearby landowners? Did someone object to the city pushing out this far into the countryside?"

"Dad wrangled with the owner for a while over the price but in the end both parties approved of the agreement."

"Maybe. I'll need the previous owner's name and contact info."

"I think Leroy's already checked that out."

"Leroy?" She jacked a doubtful eyebrow. "The local police officer?"

Sawyer's easygoing nature disappeared. He bristled, eyes narrowed. "Leroy's a good cop and a great friend. He's done his best on this."

Here was another new side to Mr. Charm. Loyalty, willing to stand up for a friend.

"I didn't mean that as an insult. Leroy does a good job, but he's short-staffed, and a growing town stretches him to the limit. He could have missed something."

She raised the camera and snapped. A line of woods and a small creek flowed to the south of the houses. "This location is beautiful. I see the appeal. Do kids play in that creek?"

"Sure. It's very shallow. Perfect for tadpole fishing." He paused. "Ever been?"

She glanced at the sky, a pretty blue dabbled with cotton-ball clouds and with an egg-yolk sun perched halfway between morning and noon.

She wouldn't play his game. They were not friends having a chitchat.

"The only thing I'm fishing for is clues."

"You don't like to fish? To cast a lure in the water and get mocked by big, fat bass that swim around your line and laugh?" He made a casting motion and began to reel. With his left hand, she noticed. "And maybe, just maybe, if you hold your mouth right, you catch one off guard and—" He yanked back on his imaginary rod, pretending to battle a fighting fish. Suddenly his shoulders dipped and he relaxed. "Rats. Lost him."

She bit back a laugh.

Sawyer Buchanon was fun. No wonder women loved him. Caution would be her friend around this man.

"I haven't been fishing in years," she said. "Not since my brothers and I used to go to the lake on weekends. We'd rent a boat at the marina and play all day." Just the three of them, away from the stress of home. She smiled a little at the memory.

"Good memories, huh?" Sawyer's focus was on her face, interested. And she liked the feeling. "Do you water-ski?"

"I haven't in a long time. Do you?"

He tapped his chest. "King of the waves. Until Brady decides to make a sharp U-turn and dump me in the brink."

"That's mean."

"No, that's fun. The trick is to pay close attention so he can't lose me and, of course, to maneuver with my mad skills and precision—" He laughed to lessen the brag. "Challenge is the Buchanon way."

"I see what you mean. It sounds like fun." And she'd not allowed herself much fun in a long time. Oh, she went out with friends, had dinner and saw movies, but the outdoors had been her love as a kid. "You and your family spend a lot of time together? All of you?"

"Lots of time. We're our favorite people." His gaze slid over her. "I imagine you were good. At water-skiing, I mean."

"As a matter of fact, I was. Light and quick." She twitched an eyebrow and crossed her arms in a teasing challenge. "I think I could handle Brady's devious moves."

"I think you could, too." He grinned, his eyes all happy dancing. "Next time Brady takes the boat out, you should come with us. Two masters competing with the boat-rocking Brady."

The invitation was like ice water. What was she doing? Flirting with a client? With the kind of man she couldn't afford to like? And during an investigation, of all the inappropriate times.

She dropped her friendly stance and stiffened. "I think we should concentrate on the investigation. Which of these homes is next on our list?"

He didn't say anything for a moment, but a tiny pucker appeared between his onyx eyebrows. After a long, thoughtful pause, he pointed to a pretty cream-colored brick. "That one."

They walked toward the house in silence. She was annoyed with herself. She was here to pry into his life, not let him pry into hers. At least she'd learned some useful information during the conversation. Nothing earth shattering but his family was close, he adored his brothers and he liked to fish and ski. He was an outdoors person. Like her.

She shut that line of thinking off so fast, she got a headache. Knowing more about him was a means to an end and part of her job. Nothing personal. Nothing personal at all.

Chapter Four

Much later, when they'd made the rounds of the Huckleberry Addition, Sawyer drove them back toward town. The private investigator intrigued him. One minute, when they'd discussed fishing and he'd done his best to be his usual enchanting self, she'd actually smiled. A second later, she'd bristled like a feral tomcat.

She didn't want to like him. He'd figured out that much, but he didn't know why. He wasn't the bad guy here.

He opened the pickup door for her and helped her up into the high cab. She didn't like that either, but his mama had raised him with manners, especially around ladies. Most women ate it up like a hot fudge sundae. Jade looked as if she wanted to throat punch him.

As he drove, he answered questions all the way. She was the most inquisitive woman he'd ever encountered. But every time he'd tried to ask about her, she'd shut him down.

The sun had moved to high overhead and his belly reminded him of the long gone popcorn and doughnut. He aimed the truck down First Street and pulled in front of the Buttered Biscuit Café.

Jade leaned forward, glaring out the windshield as if he'd driven her to a nudie bar. "What are you doing?"

"Eating. Private investigators eat, don't they?"

"I can grab something later."

He got out of the truck and went around, opening her door anyway. "You won't find a better lunch than the Biscuit's. Come on. I'll buy."

"I don't need anyone to pay for my meal."

A grin twitched his lips. "We'll fight over the check after you taste Jan's coconut cream pie."

She hesitated. "Homemade?"

He had her now. "With meringue three inches tall."

She didn't smile but she *did* capitulate. "Sold."

Score one for his team.

She let him help her down, another victory of sorts, though Sawyer didn't understand why they were in a battle.

He led the way inside, nodding to friends and a cousin as he found an open table. The café, as usual, was jammed and noisy with townspeople, most of whom he knew by their first names.

Jade walked alongside him, gazing around the small space with her usual intensity.

"Memorizing Jan's signs and slogans?" Every inch of wall space was crammed with signs or plaques, most of them snarky and clever.

She pointed at one. *Plenty of people have eaten here and gone on to live nearly normal lives.* "Pretty funny."

Then why didn't she laugh? "Jan's got sass but she sure can cook."

He pulled out a chair for her and stood, patient as Job himself. She could be stubborn. He could be patient.

Her full mouth flattened but she didn't yank away the chair and make a scene. Satisfied, Sawyer took the seat across from her and folded his arms on the laminated tabletop. He enjoyed seeing her straight on. She was nice to look at.

"Anything in particular sound good to you?" he asked.

Jade took a paper napkin from the metal container and shook it onto her lap. "You have recommendations?"

Sawyer studied the tiny mole—just one—to the left of her nose. He'd never noticed how appealing one single little beauty mark could be. "Plate lunch special."

She blinked. "What is it?"

"I didn't read the sign, but whatever it is will be good."

"Okay by me."

Nice. A woman who wasn't picky about her food, though Jade Warren was picky about everything else. Well, maybe not everything and maybe the word was *prickly* instead of *picky*.

Charla, an African American waitress with every bit as much sass as Jan, slapped two plastic menus on the table. "Hiya, Sawyer."

"Hey, Charla." He waved the menus away. "Don't need those. We'll have the special."

"Good choice. Roast beef and mashed potatoes. Jan's recipe." She retrieved the unused menus. "Drinks?"

"Iced tea for me." He shot a questioning look at Jade. "You?"

"Iced tea is good. Sweet, please."

Charla scribbled on her pad. "Who's your new friend, Sawyer?"

Now, that was a dilemma. He didn't particularly want the whole town to know he was being investigated by order of his own father. "Jade Warren, meet Charla Fredrick."

The two women exchanged greetings before Charla dashed to answer the call of "Order up." A new waitress, probably Abby's replacement, moved much slower.

Sawyer made small talk about the town and the people in the café until Charla returned with their tea glasses.

"We sure miss Abby around this place," Charla said. "Have you heard from her?"

"Yep. They're having the time of their lives."

"Good. She deserves that. You tell her I got her postcard from Venice. Such a pretty place. Is little Miss Lila doing all right with her grandma and grandpa?"

Abby's four-year-old daughter was staying with Sawyer's mom and dad while the newlyweds honeymooned in Italy.

"They're spoiling her, but you know Lila. She's a ray of sunshine and easy to spoil."

"She miss her mama much?"

"They Skype every night. I think Abby is the one suffering separation pangs. Lila's in her element."

"Abby's a good mama." Charla tossed her head, swinging giant pink earrings as if she dared anyone to argue.

"The best, and we Buchanons are all suckers for Lila."

"She does that to people. Precious child."

The waitress scooted away, returning in minutes with two steaming plates that she slid with expert ease onto the table.

"Tender roast beef, mashed potatoes and gravy, green beans and hot buttery biscuits." Sawyer rubbed his hands together. "Food of the divine."

Charla perched a hand on her ample hip. "Y'all need anything else?"

"Pie later."

"Coconut?"

Sawyer flashed a victory sign. "Two."

"Got it." She hustled away again.

Jade stared, wide-eyed, at her plate. "I'll never eat all of this."

"Take a carryout box home with you." He reached for the salt and pepper. "Where are you staying anyway?"

"The Red River Roost."

Oh, not so good. "You okay there?"

"Sure. Why wouldn't I be?"

"The River Roost isn't in the best area of town."

She got that look on her face again. The one that said he should mind his own business. "I can take care of myself."

He shrugged. So she said, but if she was his sister, he'd be concerned. Not that he considered her a sister. Not even close.

He frowned at the fluffy white insides of a steaming-hot biscuit.

She didn't like him, was suspicious as all get-out, but he was fascinated by her.

Now, what did that say about him?

Jade thought she should probably tell him to mind his own business, but Sawyer knew Gabriel's Crossing and she didn't. Forewarned was forearmed. If there were problems, she needed to know.

"What's so bad about that part of town?"

"Kind of run-down. More crime. The Roost is the type of motel where—" He leaned back in his chair and scrunched his face. "How do I put this delicately?"

"No need. I understand your point." She lifted a fork, not letting him see that his words troubled her. Not for herself, but for that lonely teen and her baby. "I was a police officer before becoming a private detective. I'm well trained, and like I said, I can take care of myself."

Sometimes she'd made a mess of things, but she'd survived and grown wiser from the experience. She didn't need or trust anyone's protection but her own.

Sliding her fork into the potatoes, she prepared to enjoy what appeared to be a delicious meal. Sawyer, she noted, had yet to begin. She shot him a questioning look. "Something wrong?"

One side of his mouth quirked up. "Grace."

"Oh." She lowered her fork and bowed her head but kept one eye on the man across the table, bracing for a major show so everyone in the place would know how devout he was.

Sawyer discreetly murmured a few words followed with "Amen." As he opened his eyes, she sat back, studying him while battling the slight guilt that she'd been focused on the man instead of the blessing.

When she'd left home, she'd left her faith behind. Not that she'd ever had much to begin with. She wasn't mad at God or anything like that. She was just…tired of the hassle.

But Sawyer Buchanon didn't fit her concept of loud, judgmental Christians. Those she knew and understood. This quiet faith, offered up with a smile and courtesy, bewildered her.

"What?"

She shook her head. "Nothing really."

"I offended you by praying?" Those magnificent eyes were serious but not apologetic. Could a man really have eyelashes that long and black?

"No. Your faith is your business."

"I take it you're not a believer?"

"Religion isn't my thing."

"Did I mention religion?" He tilted his head in the cutest way.

"Religion. Christianity. Same thing."

She took up her fork again and tasted a bite of tender roast beef and fought to suppress a moan. She'd always been an auditory eater, and this was seriously delicious.

Sawyer squinted at her, the fork in his left hand paused above the steaming, aromatic food. "Not hardly."

"What do you mean?"

"Religions are about rules and laws. Christianity is about my personal relationship with Jesus."

She'd heard that before but all this personal relationship stuff went right over her head. She knew faith didn't work like that. Her daddy had religion and claimed to be a Christian. She couldn't see the difference. *Do this. Don't do that.* If she stepped out of line, God would get her and she would suffer.

All she knew about faith was that her father twisted Bible verses to control his wife and kids.

If that was Christianity, she didn't want any part of it. Or any part of another smiling, handsome man who claimed, like Cam had, to be a man of faith.

Sawyer, quick mind that he was, instantly caught her anti-religion vibe. Somebody or something had turned her off the Lord. To him, and to every Buchanon old enough to think, her reaction was tragic. All the more because he liked her.

Something beneath the surface of the cool, serious PI intrigued him. She was much more than she'd let him see.

Yeah, and he must be sniffing too much sawdust.

Whatever. He'd take Mom's sage advice and live his faith instead of preaching it.

With that in mind, he shifted easily to her other interesting statement. "How long were you a cop?"

She sipped her tea, and for a second Sawyer thought she would tell him to mind his own business. Again.

She set the glass down and rubbed damp fingers on her napkin. In this heat, the tea glass condensed faster than Campbell's soup.

"Four years in Paris. Texas, not France."

Was that the hint of a real smile he spotted dancing around her pretty mouth? Being a naturally happy guy, he couldn't help offering a smile in response.

Apparently, discussing her job was preferable to talking about God.

"You've probably had to say that a million times."

"At least. Mostly on the phone. People here in Texoma land know the *real* Paris is in Texas."

A joke. They were making progress. Pepped him right up. "Did you like being a cop?"

"Loved it. Most of the time."

"Then why switch careers?"

"Oh, you know." She shrugged, contemplating a biscuit and a pat of real butter. "Did you always want to be a carpenter?"

Changing topics. Nice diversion. Or was that a cop tactic to dig for info?

"No. When I was six I wanted to be Batman. Still do, but they tell me the job is taken."

A spark lit her eyes. "Your degree is in business."

He slapped a hand against his chest, pretending shock. "Are you saying Batman didn't have a business plan?"

This time she actually smiled. And the result

knocked his socks off. He was tempted to look under the table to see if they were still there. Except he was wearing work boots.

"Seriously. Why a business degree if you planned to build things?"

"Dad was a stickler. All of us kids had to at least try college—preferably his alma mater, Tech. I liked college life and stuck around to get a degree." Mostly because of the good times, but he didn't tell her that part. "Even if I pound nails for the family company, I'm still a businessman. What about you? Did you attend college?"

He held his breath waiting for the cold shoulder.

"Community college classes in criminal justice and then police academy and some investigation courses. I always knew what I wanted to do."

"How does one know such a thing? Especially you, being a woman." He held up both hands. "No insult intended, but you've probably taken some flack as a female in a male-dominated field."

She stiffened up. "I can handle myself."

"No doubt." One blast of that arctic stare and a lesser man would freeze in his tracks. "But it couldn't be easy."

"I had some run-ins. Guys who didn't want to ride with me. Who thought I couldn't hold my own and would get them killed. Suggestive cartoons in my locker. The basic hazing stuff."

A bite of green beans froze halfway to Sawyer's mouth. "Say that again."

She shrugged. "Harassment made me tougher. I wasn't about to wimp out after that."

"Still." He didn't like the idea of some creep shooting innuendoes in her direction. He and the brothers would bust some chops if anyone did that to their sisters. Which brought to mind her family.

"Didn't your brothers want to knock some heads?"

Her gaze was cool. "I didn't tell them. Why would I?"

A revealing confession. She faced the world on her own. "Because men stand up for their women."

"Let's get this straight, Mr. Buchanon. I don't need or want a man to take care of me." She tossed a wadded napkin onto the table. "Not now. Not ever."

Ouch. Raw nerve. Somebody had done a number on her. Somebody who needed a knot jerked in his neck.

Sawyer was normally a lover, not a fighter, but he wouldn't mind meeting up with the culprit. Preferably alone.

Chapter Five

The next evening Jade pushed back from the small wobbly, laminated motel desk and read over the notes she'd typed into a computer document.

She'd spent the day interviewing the rest of the Buchanon family, including Dawson, who reminded her constantly of his twin. They were both too good looking for words, but so very different in personality. To her consternation, it was the playboy twin she couldn't stop thinking about.

A psychological default, she suspected, and one which she would fight with all her might. She refused to be a stereotype, falling for the same kind of man over and over again.

Dawson had been her focus today. Sawyer could wait, though she would have to talk to him again soon, regardless of her misgivings. Dan Buchanon wanted her focus on Sawyer, and the big boss was the man paying the bill.

With seven Buchanon siblings and the two parents, she'd asked the standard questions and written a lot of notes, but nothing raised a red flag. Whoever was vandalizing the Buchanon properties covered their tracks well. At this point, she needed a clue. Any clue. Sawyer had been little help.

With a sigh, she clicked Save and spent a few minutes checking social media and public records. At Sawyer's Facebook page, she paused to read tags and new entries, not missing the number of women posting. He joked around a lot, posting silly memes and photos of his family, including one of a small girl with a walker. The dark-haired cutie with the infectious smile must be Lila, Brady's stepdaughter, the child with spina bifida.

Sawyer said the family doted on the little girl, which made sense. Any family with seven kids must enjoy children.

Her thoughts went to the teenage girl and baby in Unit One. Who doted on them? No one, it seemed. Sad. Troubling.

By the time she'd returned to the motel last night, their lights had been off and she'd left them undisturbed. This morning, she'd departed the motel early for an appointment.

Technically the teen and her baby weren't Jade's business, but she'd been a police officer. She didn't back away from getting involved.

Everybody had to eat, and right now, her quick drive-through lunch was gone. Today had not been a repeat of yesterday's impromptu lunch with Sawyer at the Buttered Biscuit, though the only reason she cared was the great food, *not* the company.

Since the motel operator had kept his promise and brought over a microwave and mini fridge, she decided on a trip to the grocery store. The appliances were tiny but serviceable and would save her money in the long run. Brownie points with her boss.

She stashed the laptop under the mattress and stepped outside. The heat had eased, as if the sun had turned off the torch. In another thirty minutes, the evening air would be pleasant.

A car pulled beneath the office awning and a man and woman, both in sunglasses, got out. The woman kept her head down and hustled inside while the man glanced around as if afraid of being seen.

They weren't the first clandestine couple she'd observed sneaking into the motel. And from the number of come-and-go visitors to Unit Six, she suspected something shady, probably drugs or prostitution, was happening there.

Sawyer had been right about the area. She supposed every town had its back-alley section. Another reason to worry about Bailey and Ashton.

She was about to walk the short distance to Bailey's unit when her cell phone vibrated. Seeing the caller ID, Jade answered before the second buzz.

Breath tight in her chest, she blurted, "Mama? Are you all right?"

"I'm fine, honey." Tammy Clifton *sounded* fine. But was she really?

Since moving away from her childhood home—escaping would be the better term—Jade worried about her mother, but no amount of talk convinced Tammy Clifton to leave the Oklahoma town where she'd grown up. Southview was all she'd ever known, and fear held her there. Lots of fear.

"Are you sure? Is Daddy—"

Tammy interrupted quickly, "He's at work."

"Where?" In the past ten years, Hugh Clifton had been unemployed more often than not. This was, of course, the fault of every Buchanon who walked the face of God's green earth.

"Four Seasons Nursing Home. Maintenance."

Jade hoped the employment would last, though she heard the reservation in her mother's voice. The seeds of hope sprang eternal in Tammy Clifton but there were less of them with each passing year. "That's great."

"How are you, sweetie? When are you coming home?"

Never. Not if she could help it. Not after the fiasco last Christmas. "When are you coming to Paris to see my apartment?"

That answer was also never.

Her mother gave a soft laugh. "Oh, you know how it is around here."

"You could drive down by yourself, Mama. Paris isn't that far."

"Hugh would worry about me."

"Worry you'd leave and not go back." She couldn't keep the derisive tone from her voice.

"Now, Jade, don't start."

"Mama, women today don't have to put up with…the things you do."

"We're not going to discuss this. He's your father. Show some respect."

If Mama crammed *honor thy father and mother* down her throat one more time, Jade feared she'd scream.

"My generation is not as quick to give up on a marriage as yours."

So they were back to that. "You know why I left Cam."

Though there were things about the divorce her mother didn't know, things too painful to share, including the identity of the woman she'd found in her king-size bed—her favorite cousin, of all people, hideous judge of character that she'd been. She was wiser now, harder. Nobody would fool her again.

"Cam was such a good provider. He gave you the most beautiful home and car and anything else you wanted."

Jade barked a cold laugh. "He also put me in

the hospital, Mama. I don't care how much money he made."

A sound of distress carried through the phone. "We've had this conversation before. No one is perfect."

"Some are downright impossible. You know what Cam did. And I know how Daddy is. Please don't pretend with me."

"Neither your father nor Cam are the monsters you make them out to be."

Her family still believed she'd done something to ignite Cam's anger that night. She had, though she hadn't known it at the time.

Little had she realized when she'd married Cam that she was following in her mother's footsteps, from one angry man to another. That psychological defect again. Now she knew better.

"I'm sorry, Mama. I love you. Let's not fight."

"I love you, too. That's why I called. To hear my girl's voice and know you're well and happy. You are happy, aren't you, sugar?"

Desperation coated her mother's words. She wanted Jade to have what she didn't though she refused to admit how unhappy she was herself. Admitting it would mean she'd have to do something about it.

"I'm great. How are my brothers?"

"Staying busy." Her mother's way of saying she didn't see them often enough. "Robby's wife brought the baby by a few days ago. I never dreamed being a grandma would be this wonderful."

Jade's heart stood still long enough to be reminded of what she didn't have. Of what Mama didn't know.

"Twila sends me pictures on Facebook and Instagram. Jeremiah's a cutie."

"You should come home and visit more. He needs to know his auntie Jade."

Jade sighed and rubbed a now pulsing right temple. "I won't listen to Daddy harp on me about Cam or the Bible or going to church."

Or watch him treat you like a second-class servant.

"Cam was in town yesterday. He asked about you."

Ah, so now they were getting down to the real reason for the phone call. Jade's grip tightened on the cell phone. "How can you take his side?"

"I don't agree with what he did, but six years is long enough to hold a grudge."

"You're talking to me about holding a grudge? What about our family's hatred toward the Buchanons? Isn't that a grudge?"

"That's different."

"How?"

"All I'm saying is that you need to forgive. For your sake if not his. Bitterness will make you old and ugly."

Cam the creep needed to repent before he deserved forgiveness, not that she'd give it even if he crawled over flaming glass and begged. Cam Warren would get nothing from her but animosity. Ever.

Rather than argue, she looked for a reason to end the conversation.

"Mama, I'm sorry to cut this short but I'm working a new case."

"Oh? Anything exciting?"

If you knew, you'd disown me.

"I can't discuss an ongoing investigation. Privacy issues and all that. Gotta run now. I'll call you tomorrow."

"Don't call during meal times. You know how that aggravates Hugh."

"I know, Mama. I know." *Walk on egg shells. Sacrifice your soul, your pride and your self-esteem. Anything to keep the peace.* "Bye now."

Disheartened but resigned, she ended the call.

Talking to her family always tied her in knots and left her feeling vaguely guilty. She wouldn't be able to relax for hours now.

Sliding the phone into her pocket, she started back inside her room but paused, gazing at Bailey's closed door.

She hadn't seen the girl yesterday or today. Was she okay? Did she need anything? Did the baby?

With determined strides she closed the short distance between rooms and knocked.

The door opened in seconds. With an inner

groan, Jade shook her head. The girl needed some lessons in self-defense.

Cop instinct took over. "Never open this door without asking who's on the other side."

"Oh." Bailey's eyes widened. "I didn't think."

"Not thinking can get you raped. Or killed. And then what would happen to Ashton?"

"I'm sorry." Head down, the girl's voice was whisper quiet, her distress obvious.

Jade reined in the lecture. She touched Bailey's shoulder. "I apologize for coming on strong, but you need to be more careful."

"Okay. I will. I promise. Sometimes I'm so stupid."

"Don't get down on yourself. We all mess up sometimes." Jade offered a smile to ease the strain. "I'm driving to the store. Want to come along?"

Bailey brightened. "Sure. Ashton and me are sick of this room."

She could only imagine. A little one needed space to move and play.

"We'll grab some sandwich fixings and stop at the park. How does that sound?"

The offer was a spur-of-the-moment thought but why not? Being a Good Samaritan was in a cop's blood, and the distraction might help to clear her mind so she could come up with a clue for the investigation.

"That would be awesome. Ashton loves the park but it's so far to walk. He's getting heavy."

"No stroller?"

Bailey shook her head. "A friend said she'd give me hers, but then she got pregnant again."

Jade kept her thoughts to herself as she took the baby from Bailey's arms and waited for the girl to grab a bottle and a diaper and follow her to the car. Bailey's flip-flops slapped the concrete.

They chatted companionably during the trip and Jade couldn't help digging for information about Bailey's family, her life, the high school she hadn't finished. She didn't know the local system but surely someone could help this kid and her baby.

When they arrived at the park, Jade pulled her emergency blanket from the trunk for Ashton to play on while the women organized their impromptu picnic on the concrete table. Over Bailey's protest, she'd bought baby food and a banana for Ashton and far more groceries than she'd intended.

They were finishing their sandwiches when a big maroon pickup truck pulled into the parking area next to Jade's car.

Her heart jumped. She stared. Was that Sawyer's truck? And if so, what was he doing here?

Sawyer leaned over the steering wheel and squinted toward two women sitting at a concrete picnic table beneath one of the huge pecan trees shading the city park. He'd thought the Chevy Cruze looked like Jade's and sure enough there she was, having a picnic.

That he also recognized her companion convinced him to hop out of the truck and say hello. Not that he needed much convincing, but it was nice to have Bailey as an excuse. Miss Sherlock Holmes had been on his mind all day and he'd not seen her one time. That he missed talking to her after yesterday's interrogations said he might have a loose board in the attic.

The thought made him chuckle. He, a carpenter, with a loose board. Better take a nail gun to that.

He sauntered across the grass, still vivid green from a recent cloudburst. Inside the shady park, the temperature dropped ten degrees, and he removed his sunglasses, hanging them on his shirt pocket.

As he reached the table, Bailey rose, Coke can in hand. "Sawyer? I thought that was you. Hi."

Jade, he noted, cut a sharp look between them. After her insistence that he was some kind of womanizer, she probably thought the worst. But she was way out of line there. He wasn't a womanizer and even if he was, Bailey was only a kid.

"Hey, Bailey. Long time no see. Where you been? We've missed you at Life Group."

Bailey turned three shades of crimson and lifted a baby from a pallet next to the table. "Oh, you know. After I had Ashton, I was kind of busy and…"

Her voice trailed away and Sawyer, being an astute sort of guy, caught the drift. The older boyfriend no one in their church's youth group had trusted must have skipped out and left her with a baby. And she was too embarrassed to come to church, expecting judgment. Sawyer hated that. Church should be the place to run to, not from, but he understood Bailey's anxiety. Some people who called themselves Christians could use a good dose of Jesus's love.

"Let me see that little fella."

Had he known about the baby? He couldn't remember for sure. And if he had heard, he felt like a jerk for not following up. As young as she was, Bailey needed church support more than ever.

She handed over the little one. Ashton gurgled, drooling a little, and patted Sawyer's face with a slobbery hand.

He laughed. "Anointed in baby drool."

Bailey laughed nervously. "I'm really sorry. He's cutting a tooth, I think."

"Let me see." Sawyer tugged the baby's bottom lip and peered inside. "Yep. Bottom gums are puffy and red. I think I see a little tooth bud down there."

Jade cut into the conversation, a slight dip in her forehead. "You two know each other?"

Bailey nodded. "Church youth group. Sawyer's one of the leaders."

"Really?"

From the chill in her voice, Jade was not impressed—whether with church or him, he had yet to figure out. Maybe both.

"Yeah," Bailey said. "He does a great job."

"No work required. I get to hang out with teenagers and have fun. Who wouldn't want to do that?" Sawyer eased a hip onto the table, still bouncing the baby. He was a cute little critter with big brown eyes, pale, barely there hair and an easy nature. "Nice evening for a picnic."

Bailey pointed to the food spread on the table. "Would you like a sandwich?" She shot a look toward Jade. "If it's okay with Jade, I mean. She bought the stuff."

The PI didn't exactly look enthusiastic but she waved a hand toward the various foods scattered across the table. "If you haven't eaten…"

Sawyer heard the hesitation and because he wanted to ruffle her feathers, he grinned. "I haven't. A sandwich sounds good."

He handed the baby back to Bailey and accepted a baby wipe in return. "He's a dandy, Bailey. Bring him to youth group on Wednesday. Introduce him."

Hope flared in the teen's eyes, but she only said, "I'll think about it."

After a minute, she carried Ashton to the swings a few yards away.

Sawyer swung his legs over the concrete bench and began rummaging in the sandwich fixings. Pepper jack, his favorite cheese. Shaved ham. Good choices.

Jade held out two slices of wheat bread. Sawyer took them and hoped for mayo.

"I didn't see you around today. Dawson said you interviewed him." He'd started to say *interrogated* but suspected the term might cause a cold front to move in.

She wasn't exactly warm but she hadn't kicked him out of the park, either. And she was feeding him. He must be making progress. The fact that he wanted to still befuddled him.

"Along with the rest of your family." She offered a squeeze bottle of mustard.

He shook his head. No mayo. He'd survive. "Learn anything useful?"

"No." The reply came with a frustrated sigh.

"It's early in the investigation yet. Don't get discouraged."

"You were the one who said I wouldn't find anything Leroy and the fire investigators hadn't."

"Yeah, well. I might have been grumpy. You caught me before I'd had my caffeine."

"I'll remember that."

While he chowed down on the ham and cheese, she zipped open a pack of Oreos and took one.

The squeak of swing chains drew his attention. He glanced at Bailey, sitting in the swings with the baby on her lap. One foot tapped the ground, moving them back and forth in a steady rhythm. She was only a kid. With a kid.

He finished his bite and swallowed. "How did you and Bailey connect?"

"She's living at the Red River Roost."

He jacked an eyebrow. "With who? Baby's daddy?"

He had a very clear memory of the boy she'd dated. Though he and others had tried to mentor the young man, the boy had been a loser, a thug with an attitude and no interest in changing.

"Alone. Her mom kicked her out of the house and the boyfriend disappeared. No job. No education. I don't want to think about what her life is going to be. Doesn't this town have resources for kids like her?"

Jade nibbled the edge of a cookie. Chocolate crumbs specked her upper lip. Sawyer had a remedy for that but he didn't figure she'd appreciate his thoughtfulness.

The woman distracted him something fierce.

"If it doesn't it should. Bailey used to attend youth group but when she started hanging out with an older boy, she stopped coming around."

One of the leaders should have followed up. *He* should have talked to her, but he usually left the girls up to the female leaders.

"She said he wouldn't let her."

Sawyer blinked toward Bailey and then met Jade's stormy gaze. "Wouldn't *let her* attend church?"

Her nostrils flared, the pouty mouth tight. "Typical male. The creep. It's all about what they want, never about the girl."

"Not all men are like that, Jade. No *real* man is."

With a huff, she crossed her arms. If she didn't have cookie crumbs on her face, she'd be scary. "Right."

Sawyer made a mental note. *Distrustful of the male species.*

He glanced at her left hand even though he knew from a sneak peek yesterday that she wore no rings. "Is that why you're not married? Too many creeps?"

"Let's just say once burned was plenty for me. I'm divorced." She uncrossed her arms and reached for another Oreo. "Thankfully."

Her pronouncement didn't surprise him. But beneath the defiance and anger, he detected hurt.

Someone had hurt her, and though she wasn't a bit of his business, seeing her pain made him mad.

Chapter Six

The next day Jade felt about as confused as a rat in a new maze. After she had basically labeled Sawyer and the entire male gender as nothing but user creeps, he had changed the subject as if not a bit insulted. The man was…baffling.

During a long conversation about the small town of Gabriel's Crossing, the investigation, and silly twin tricks he and Dawson had contrived to confuse people, she'd found herself warming a teeny bit. Maybe more than that.

"He definitely earned his reputation as a charmer," she muttered. She'd have to be careful not to lose her objectivity.

"Excuse me? Did you say something?"

Jade whirled toward the voice. Sawyer's pregnant sister, Allison, had come into the Buchanon Built conference room where Jade was plowing through piles of old records, some on the computer and others in file boxes. Except for Quinn

Buchanon, who had bailed five minutes after her arrival muttering about working at home, she'd been alone for the better part of an hour.

"Sorry. Talking to myself."

"Don't apologize. I do it, too." Allison Hamilton patted her slightly round tummy. "Only now, Junior has to listen."

Jade allowed a smile though she knew the effort looked pinched. "Boy or girl?"

"We don't know yet. Whichever God sends will be a wonderful blessing."

A hollow ache started up. "No preference?"

"Well." The brunette shrugged one shoulder. The woman glowed. Glistened. "Between you and me, I'd love a little cowboy like his daddy. And I really want to decorate the nursery in cute little ponies and cartoon cows."

"No reason you can't do that for a girl."

"True, but if I have a girl, Jake has already decreed her a princess."

Jade's stomach tightened. Naturally, and Jake would get his way.

Rather than spew her negative thoughts, she turned back to the pile of records. Allison came alongside the table and peered at the stack.

"Finding anything useful?"

"Not really. Your family runs a tight ship. Few consumer complaints. Most of those required only minor adjustments."

"My dad is a stickler. He goes ballistic if one

of the boys or a subcontractor messes up. Subs know Dad won't use them again unless the finished project is near perfection."

"Has he fired many?"

"A few."

Jade made a mental note. Someone surely resented a tough, exacting boss. Someone besides her father.

A moment of angst gripped her. Her father and the Buchanons had parted ways years ago. If Dad had wanted revenge, he'd have taken it long before now. Besides, he was an hour away and never came to Gabriel's Crossing. No way he could be involved.

"Can you think of any subcontractors who might hold a grudge?" *Please don't say my father.*

"Oh, that's why I came in here in the first place." Allison produced a manila folder. "Dad dropped this off for you. He said he and Mom had brainstormed some additional names and situations last night."

"Great." Jade accepted the folder, eager to dig in. Maybe this would be the info that broke the case wide open. She placed the folder on the table but, not wanting to be rude, left it unopened.

Allison crossed to the refrigerator in the far corner, reached in and took out an orange. With a sheepish shrug she said, "I'm starving all the time lately."

"I've heard that's normal."

"No kids?"

That hollow ache deepened. "No kids. Not married."

"Oh. Well, I highly recommend it—with the right guy." She peeled the orange with her fingers, sending up a strong citrus scent to compete with the lumber and coffee smells of the conference room. "If you're in the market, I happen to have two single brothers. Good looks. Good guys."

The jury was still out on the good guys part. Though she had to admit Sawyer had made a dint in her animosity last night at the park when he'd bounced Bailey's baby around and hadn't complained about being drooled on. Cam would have freaked out. Sawyer actually seemed to enjoy himself and he was genuinely concerned about Bailey.

Was there more to him than a pretty face and a flirty grin?

Interesting question, and one she would follow up on. For the case.

Jade responded to Allison's not-so-subtle matchmaking hint with an insincere smile. "Conflict of interest. I am investigating your single brothers."

Allison waved off the idea. "Dad is spitting in the wind on that."

"You think so? Then who should be the focus? Who's causing the problem?"

"I wish I knew." The pregnant woman reached

back into the fridge, grabbed a carton of milk and another orange and said, "Hope you find something," before leaving the room.

Five minutes later she did. And the discovery nearly gave her a heart attack.

Her father's name, big and bold, next to Clifton Concrete, the name of his now defunct company, jumped off the list of lawsuits Buchanon Built had filed.

Pulse thumping, she frowned at the information. A lawsuit? Against her father? Dad had never mentioned a lawsuit. He'd said the Buchanons refused to pay for work rendered and bad-mouthed him to the other contractors. According to Hugh Clifton, Dan Buchanon was a wicked man who played favorites and discriminated against persons of true faith.

She couldn't ask her father for the whole story, either. He'd want to know why. Worse, if the Buchanons found out she was related to anyone on this list of possible suspects, she'd be in big trouble. Her boss, Dale, would take her off the case. He might even fire her for withholding that all-important piece of the puzzle.

She gnawed on her lip, thinking. She was a PI. She needed more information on what happened with her father. But she'd have to be very subtle or risk raising suspicions.

Folder in hand, she stepped out into the office area. Jaylee tapped away at her computer while

Allison spoke to her mother. Karen Buchanon, an attractive blonde with a warm personality, looked up when Jade came into the room.

Choosing her words carefully, Jade said, "I have a question about some of the lawsuits on your list."

By asking about more than one, she shouldn't raise any red flags.

Moving to Karen's side, she pointed out several, asking astute questions. Any of these contractors, she told herself, stood as much chance of being the culprit as her father.

When she came to Hugh Clifton, she continued in her cool, professional manner, sounding, at least to her ears, completely objective.

Karen's pretty forehead puckered. "Clifton. Yes, I remember that contractor. Dan and I discussed him last night. His workmanship was shoddy, and he used cut-rate materials but charged us for top-of-the-line. At first, we didn't know about the cut corners. He was crafty. He made everything appear legit and had good references."

Jade's stomach sank. "Which you checked?"

"Yes. Apparently, he'd once run a reputable business in Oklahoma, but when the foundations of several new homes started shifting, Dan filed a lien, hoping the man would do the honorable thing and make repairs. When he refused, claiming financial problems, we had no choice but to take him to court."

"Foundations shifted?" Jade's stomach dipped

low. This was not good. Not good at all. "Isn't that dangerous?"

"Absolutely. In the end, we were forced to demolish all four homes Clifton Concrete had worked on, and you can imagine how costly that was to everyone. We had to work very hard to keep our reputation as a trusted builder from being ruined."

"Didn't his company have insurance?"

"He defaulted on that, too, apparently. Nonpayment. The man had gambling issues, I believe, and was desperate for money."

Her holier-than-thou father gambled? Why had she not known this?

"Interesting." She was too stunned to say much else at this point. She needed to get away and breathe deep, to process.

"We never like to take a contractor to court," Karen continued, "but someone could have been badly injured in those homes. Not that the lawsuit recouped much of our loss."

Now she understood why her father's business had failed, why he'd sold everything he could and filed for bankruptcy. And why he hated the Buchanons. He blamed them so he wouldn't have to blame himself. And to keep his gambling secret.

Did Mama know? Should Jade tell her?

Rubbing a hand over her now aching forehead, Jade recognized the conflict of interest, but now, more than ever, she wanted to see this investigation through. She must discover if her father was involved in the Buchanon break-ins. Not for his sake. For her mother's.

Sawyer hummed a happy little tune as he yanked on the always stuck door leading into the Buchanon Built warehouse. The heavy metal screeched on its hinges, high-pitched and painful. Sawyer winced. He needed to fix that.

The screech turned two faces in his direction. His mom's and...*hers*. The PI tickling his thoughts.

He'd seen Jade's car parked outside. He knew she was here, digging into Buchanon business, courtesy of his father. As aggravating as the intrusion was, he didn't blame Jade. She was only doing her job. That she was also prickly and frosty at times only served to heighten his interest—odd duck that he was.

"Nancy Drew." He moseyed toward the big central desk where his two sisters, his mom and the PI were hanging out. "How goes the investigation?"

Jade looked good, but then she'd looked good in that scalding black suit the first day they'd met. Miserable, but intriguing and oh so neat and professional. Last night at the park, in cuffed jean shorts and a pink T-shirt, she'd been downright human.

Very human.

"Progressing slowly." Did he perceive a slight

thawing in her steady gaze? "You and I need to talk again soon. About the case, I mean."

Sweet. She *was* thawing. Things were looking up.

"I'm free this weekend." As soon as the words were out, he bounced a fist against his forehead. "No, wait. I almost forgot. I have plans."

Those finely tuned eyebrows lifted like the golden arches. "Big date?"

"The biggest. Four beautiful women at once, all who love me."

Three of those women burst out laughing. They never let him get away with anything.

"Sawyer," his mother chided. "Stop teasing her. Jade doesn't know how to take you yet."

Allison leaned over the U-shaped counter, her short hair flying around her pert and, of late, rounded face. "What Sawyer means, Jade, is that the family is going to the lake together on Saturday and he happens to have three sisters and a mom who love him *in spite* of everything." Allison splayed four fingers.

"Oh. I see. Four women." Jade did not look impressed.

"Don't pay any attention to him." Allison waved him off as if he were a gnat. "He's trying to endear himself with his juvenile sense of humor but failing miserably."

"Hey!" Sawyer pretended hurt. "See if I bring you any more doughnuts."

Allison came over and patted his cheek. "You will feed me. I know you will. You love me and I love you, Sawyer Mark."

He grabbed her in a gentle hug. "Got that right, cutie. Even if you are getting fat."

Allison laughed happily, bracketing her tiny tummy pooch.

He loved seeing his little sister this way, in love and expecting Jake's baby with so much joyful anticipation that she almost had Sawyer wishing he could find the right woman to marry.

Jaylee looked up from her computer. "What are you doing this weekend, Jade? You won't be working on the case, will you?"

"I will if anything new comes to light."

"Why not come to the lake with us? When the Buchanons are relaxed they talk more. Never know what little thing you might learn."

"I couldn't intrude on family time."

"You wouldn't be intruding." Now that Jaylee had come up with the idea, Sawyer jumped on it. "We take friends and colleagues all the time."

"All work and no play," Allison said, and Sawyer secretly blessed her. "Fun is guaranteed."

"Well, I don't know..."

He could see she was weakening, so he tossed in a hook loaded with bait.

"Jade skis," he said to his mother. "She thinks she can handle Brady's moves."

Allison paused in peeling an orange. "You ski?"

"Well, I used to. It's been a long time."

"Like riding a bike. Muscle memory." Sawyer held both hands in front of him in water-ski position. "Brady's boat, skis, big water."

"But Brady's not back from his honeymoon."

"And guess who has his keys?" Sawyer tapped his chest. "Can you handle *my* moves?"

He realized how that sounded but didn't back down. Jade's gray eyes sparked at the challenge and maybe at the innuendo, too. "I think I can. The question is, can you handle mine?"

"Ah, the gauntlet has been thrown, the die cast, the challenge laid." He rubbed his hands together. "Bring it on, Sherlock."

To his disappointment, Jade was already shaking her head. Fluffy, pretty blond hair swished around her shoulders like a pale cloud.

"Thank you for the invitation but maybe another time. It sounds terrific, but I promised to hang out with Bailey on Saturday."

"Bring her along!" He glanced toward his mother. He'd told her about Bailey's situation, hoping she knew of resources to help the girl. "Right, Mom?"

Mom, bless her, was always on his side. "If Bailey's stuck in a motel room with a baby all day, she'll probably thrill at the chance for some recreation."

"I hadn't thought of that." But Jade was thinking about it now. He could tell by that tiny wrinkle in her pretty forehead.

"She's a teenager." Sawyer shamelessly used the girl to break down Jade's resistance. Was a skiing challenge really so important? "Bailey needs to have fun and we Buchanons are a regular fun-mobile. As well as a willing bunch of built-in babysitters. You would be doing Bailey and Ashton a favor."

"Well—" Her teeth caught her full bottom lip, gnawed a little. Such a pretty lip.

And she was weakening.

"Look at it this way, Jade. You get to help Bailey, ask us a million questions and have a terrific day on the lake with perhaps the greatest family this side of the Red River—unless you're afraid you can't live up to the Sawyer ski challenge."

He saw the smiles on his sisters' faces. They knew him too well and would probably give him a hard time about his persistence. He didn't care. Miss Magnum PI was a tough cookie, but after watching her with Bailey and Ashton, he suspected she had a very soft heart. One that he wanted to know better.

So he let the bait dangle. "Come on. What do you say? Help out a needy teenager. Stuff your face on Dad's barbecue. Battle my mad boating skills."

Without cracking a smile, Jade pointed a finger at him. "Since you put it that way, practice your driving, mister, because you're on."

Chapter Seven

The moment she told Bailey about the lake trip Jade stopped regretting her decision to go. The girl was ecstatic. You would think she'd won a trip to Disney World.

"This is the best day ever, Jade." Bailey bounced around the hotel room like the teenager she was, packing a backpack for Ashton. She'd been this way for two days. Jubilant. Planning. Behaving as if she'd never had a day of fun in her life.

Maybe she hadn't.

Jade settled in the one motel room chair with Ashton and a formula bottle while they talked. "I bought sunscreen and a little hat for Ashton yesterday."

She'd also intended to buy a new swimsuit, but Bailey bemoaned the fact that since Ashton's birth hers no longer fit and she couldn't afford a new one, so they'd both decided to wear shorts and tank tops. Ashton would be fine in a onesie.

Bailey paused in her mad packing to anxiously twist the end of her ponytail. "I hadn't even considered that. What if Ashton gets sunburned?"

"We'll be extra careful to slather him with this and then keep him in the shade as much as possible. Sawyer said the Buchanons bring the house, including an awning, a grill, chairs, you name it."

"They are so awesome." Bailey stuffed yet another diaper into the backpack. She had enough to stay a week. "Are you and Sawyer, like, a couple or something?"

The question blindsided Jade. She blinked at the girl until the question registered. "What? Sawyer and me? No. He's a client."

"Oh. I thought, after the park and now the lake, he must be crushing on you."

Jade laughed humorlessly. The idea of Sawyer crushing on her when he had a bevy of beauties vying for his attentions was ludicrous. The fact that this knowledge bothered her set alarms clanging. She knew better. He was the exact kind of man she would not fall for again. Shallow. Self-focused. Charming to a fault. Jade was determined that he would not think she agreed to the lake trip because of him. The trip was to enhance the investigation and for Bailey.

That she was almost as excited as Bailey was beside the point.

She checked the time on her cell phone. "He'll be here soon. Are you about ready?"

The question was barely out of her mouth when a heavy knock vibrated the door. Bailey rushed forward as if to let the caller in.

"Bailey. Caution."

"Right." The teen slowed to a walk, wiped her hands down the sides of her shorts before calling out, "Who is it?"

A muffled voice came through the door. "The chauffeur. Your carriage awaits."

Bailey yanked the door wide, giggling. "Sawyer, you're so funny."

Jade didn't roll her eyes but she wanted to. She'd recognized Sawyer's voice too but the teen had a long way to go to be street savvy.

Sawyer stepped into the room. Something in the center of Jade's chest reacted. Even baggy cargo shorts and a well-worn Red Raiders T-shirt didn't detract from his looks. But it was the way he greeted Bailey that really got her thinking. Like a big brother. The way he greeted his sisters.

He casually flopped a muscled arm over the teen's shoulders, gave a quick squeeze and released her with a cheery smile. "All ready for a great day?"

Bailey turned every shade of red known to humans. "I can't wait. I'm so excited."

No female, it seemed, was impervious to Sawyer Buchanon.

Except Jade. Even if he had a kind side—and he did—and even if she found him attractive—

and who wouldn't—he was a Buchanon. And her maiden name was on his father's naughty list.

He spotted her inside the dim room with the baby and raised both palms in a comical, supplicating gesture.

"What's this? You've ditched me for a younger man?"

"His toothless grin was irresistible."

Sawyer paused for one second as if her return banter caught him off guard. She knew he considered her humorless and cold, which was for the best, but she wasn't always that way.

Crossing the room, Sawyer swooped Ashton into his arms. "You ladies ready? Where's the squirt's bag?"

Bailey reached for the backpack but Sawyer beat her to it, swung it over his opposite shoulder, and the four of them headed out for the day.

The sight of the man with a baby in his tanned, muscled arms tugged at Jade's insides. He was a puzzle she couldn't fit into her tidy mental box.

Once they were in the truck, driving north with a glittery blue boat pulling behind, Jade turned toward him. "What about the rest of your family? Are we meeting them somewhere?"

"They left earlier, all except Jake and Allison who will come later. Mom and Dad rise with the sun and like to set up camp before everyone else arrives."

"Nice of them."

"Strategy. Broken Bow Lake usually isn't too crowded, but you never know. We have a special spot."

Jade almost swallowed her tongue.

"Broken Bow?" she managed, hoping she sounded normal.

"Ever been there? It's a gorgeous lake. Clear and deep, lots of secluded coves and little islands to play on."

"A few times." Heart pounding in her throat, she swiveled toward the passenger window and watched the passing scenery.

Broken Bow was close to Southview. Too close.

Sawyer plopped into one of the many lawn chairs beneath the shady blue awning that stretched out along a narrow section of beach. Behind their day camp, thick, pine-scented forest shielded them from the rest of the world, and in front, a little cove of blue mountain water glistened in the sun. An occasional boat motored past in the distance but for the most part only Buchanon noises melded with the lapping water.

In the nearby shallows, Brady's stepdaughter wore a bright orange life vest above a pink tutu swimsuit and splashed with Charity's son and daughter, Ryan and Amber. Little Lila and the older Amber were tight, and Ryan took his job as big, protective cousin seriously. Nonetheless, the whole family, including Sawyer, kept a close eye on Lila, the special needs child.

Out on the lake, Brady's boat sliced across the sparkling current as Quinn pulled his fiancée and Derek, her nephew, on a tube. The boy stood up in the rubber conveyance and circled one hand over his head cowboy-style to yell, "Yahoo!"

The once surly Derek, like Quinn, had come a long way in the past few months.

"Ever been tubing?" Feeling pleasantly relaxed, Sawyer slowly turned his face toward Bailey. The needy teen twitched his heart, and from the way Mom and the sisters circled her with chairs, they felt the same.

"No, but it looks fun." Ashton bounced on her lap, patting chubby little hands on his legs.

"I'll take you around when Quinn comes in."

"Really?" Her face brightened, but every bit as quickly darkened. "Oh, I better not. I can't leave Ashton."

Jade, who stood nearby talking to Dad and Dawson about the case, must have overheard. She glanced around. "You go, Bailey. Have fun. That's why you're here. I'll look after Ashton."

"We'll all watch him." Charity reached for the baby. "I've wanted to get my hands on this little doll since you arrived. My kids are growing up too fast."

"We need more babies in this family." His mother eyed him. "You and your brother need to stop dragging your feet, find a couple of nice Christian women and give me more grandchildren."

"Can't find anyone who'll have us. We're too ugly," he said lazily. But the fact that he felt Jade's eyes on him during the exchange poked at a lonely spot. Recently that spot, along with his empty town house, had started to bother him. The fact that Jade had a problem with God, or appeared to, bothered him, too.

He leaned his head back against the chaise lounge and tipped a ball cap over his eyes. He had plenty of opportunities for dates. He was never alone unless he wanted to be. So why had this sudden wave of loneliness washed over him?

Sometime later Jade was still trying to relax as she stroked coconut-scented sunscreen over her arms. Being this close to home made her anxious. She didn't want to run into family, or worse, Cam. The chances were slim that any of them would show up in this particular spot on the lake, but she couldn't be certain.

Dan Buchanon had answered a handful of questions about the lawsuits she'd been checking into, but then Karen reminded them that this was a pleasure trip, not work, and the subject was closed. Dan had sheepishly retired to his fishing reel with Quinn. A lanky boy went with them and the three male heads now huddled above a tackle box in search of the proper bait.

Out on the lake, Sawyer had taken charge of the boat and pulled a tube carrying Bailey and Jaylee. There were so many Buchanons, Jade scrambled to keep them straight, but Bailey's grin was big enough to see from here.

Pleased at the girl's delight and glad she'd agreed to this outing regardless of her family's proximity, she sipped at a bottle of cold water and scribbled in her notebook. She was safe here. Her family wouldn't know she was consorting with the enemy.

Bothered by feeling guilty when she'd done nothing wrong, she tuned in to the conversation between Charity and Karen, hoping to glean something useful to the investigation. Instead, she heard a discussion of Charity's navy pilot husband and the concern that he was once more flying in a danger zone and had missed his usual phone call home.

Sawyer guided the boat to the nearby dock and cut the engine.

"Hey, Nancy Drew, come on. Your turn." He held up a water ski.

Her insides leaped. "It's been a long time."

"Excuses, excuses." He laughed, letting her know he teased. "Admit the real truth. You fear my mad boating maneuvers."

She stowed the notepad in her tote and started

toward him. Lacing her fingers, she flipped her hands palm out and stretched like a champion warming up for the finals. "Bring it on, boat man."

Quinn hooted from the sidelines. "You better watch out, Sawyer. She looks serious."

"I'm shaking in my flip-flops."

He looked incredible standing at the boat helm, glorious eyes covered in dark shades and black hair glistening in the sunlight. A magazine ad.

He tossed her a life jacket. "Saddle up, cowgirl."

Ignoring the troubling quiver in her belly that she hoped was caused by the thought of skiing for the first time in several years and not by the man, Jade donned the jacket and waded into the shallows to put the skis on while Sawyer hooked the ski rope and prepared the boat.

The other twin ambled out onto the dock. "I'll spot for you."

A spotter. Good. For all his reckless-sounding bravado, Sawyer didn't forgo safety. She relaxed a little and hoped he was right about muscle memory.

Sawyer hitched his chin. "Ready when you are, Jade."

She settled into the water, knees bent, arms out and skis at the ready. "I demand a warm-up period."

"Got it."

She'd watched him drive the boat for Bailey and the other kids. He knew what he was doing, though their challenge loomed large in her head. Would he drive like a maniac? Would he dunk her in the brink to intentionally embarrass her and prove his masculine superiority?

The motor revved as the boat slowly began to move forward. Jade's adrenaline jacked. Her breath caught, released.

The wake lapped gently at her body, bobbing her up and down in the thick life jacket. Sawyer looked back over his shoulder and gave a thumbs-up. Grinning, she nodded, the thrill of being on the water again too good to resist as he accelerated and she began to rise.

In less than a minute she was on her feet, the wind whipping her hair as she sailed across the waves. Ten miles an hour. Twenty. Now twenty-five.

She tasted the lake spray, relished the cool air, the blinding glare of sun on water. In her peripheral vision, trees passed in a green blur.

A laugh burst free. She let out a whoop of joy.

Sawyer's head whipped around and his teeth flashed before he returned his attention to driving. He kept the speed steady, the trajectory straight, giving her time to adjust.

Quickly gaining confidence, she found her balance and began to move from side to side, only a little but enough to know she hadn't lost her skills. Living this close to the lake most of her life, she loved the water and was an accomplished swimmer, skier, boater. Sad that she'd stopped enjoying it. Until today.

She raised a thumb, indicating her desire to go faster. Her legs burned and her knees protested. She was out of shape but too stubborn and having too much fun to stop. Dawson lifted an answering thumb as he spoke to the driver. Again, Sawyer glanced over his shoulder. She raised her thumb, urging him to speed up. He seemed to consider for a second but turned back to the controls.

She was flying now, not another boat anywhere nearby. It was as though they had the lake to themselves. The twins' voices floated back to her, but she couldn't make out the words.

Though her arms ached, she thrilled to the wind, the water, the speed. Confident, she swerved the skis to the left and then the right.

The action proved too much for her out-of-practice knees. She went down.

Lake water closed over her head. Automatically—that muscle memory thing—she released the rope and bobbed to the surface.

Sawyer had already cut the throttle and turned the boat back toward her. "You all right?"

The jokester was now all business. Face serious, intent.

"Great. This is amazing!" She started to swim toward the boat.

"Save your energy. I'll bring the rope back to you." In a maneuver that appeared easy but she knew wasn't, he guided the floating ski rope to within inches of where she bobbed.

As much as she didn't want to stop, she said, "My legs are burning. I should probably go ashore for a while."

"In the boat or on the skis?"

She grinned. "The skis. I'm no wimp."

He raised his hands. "No argument from me. Hang tight. I'll have you back up in a minute."

True to his word, she was on her feet and flying again in seconds. With precision, he delivered her to shore, killed the engine and hopped out to tie up the boat.

Water sports made her ravenous and the smell of grilling hamburgers made her stomach rumble. She glanced toward the awning fifty feet up on shore where Dan had taken over the grill and some of the Buchanon women laid out side dishes on a folding table.

More exhausted than she wanted to be, Jade plopped in the shallows and began to unlatch the binding. Dawson slogged past with a fist bump. "Nice moves out there."

Rid of the skis, she was shocked by her shaky knees but proud that she'd held her own.

Sawyer leaped off the dock and flip-flopped through the water. "Not bad for a girl."

She stuck her legs straight out. Binding straps left red streaks atop her feet.

"Fighting words, boat man." She glanced up

at him, too tired and pleased to fight the pleasant hum in her bloodstream. "Why no fancy boating moves from you? I thought you had mad skills."

He shrugged a broad shoulder. "I took pity on you."

Normally, a comment like that would make her stiffen. Instead she laughed. "Coward."

"Well, yeah. But that was a warm-up. I'll get you before the day's over." He slipped into the water next to her, cargo shorts and all. Removing his flip-flops, he tossed them at the camp. They landed with a plop. "Seriously, you did good out there. I was impressed."

A happy balloon inflated in her chest. "Thanks. You made it easy. You're a very good driver."

He didn't answer, didn't even preen, and side by side they leaned back on their elbows and relaxed in the sun, water waist deep.

Two kids ran past and splashed them, squealing. They both laughed and threatened revenge.

"I need water balloons," she said, pretending to take aim at the kids.

"Spoken like a Buchanon." His grin captured hers. Something dinged in her brain, but she ignored the warning.

He was a flirt as well as a client but she was allowed to have a good time on her day off. Wasn't she?

Quinn and his fiancée, Gena, approached, holding hands. "Are you through with the boat?"

"For now. Go ahead."

"I'm going to show Gena the island." Quinn indicated a patch of green a hundred yards down the shoreline. "Want to go with us?"

Sawyer shook his head and the other pair got in the craft and motored away.

"They look happy together." Did her voice sound wistful?

"Love has changed my brother." Sawyer levered up, rubbing the sand from his elbows.

Love had changed her, too, though not in the way Sawyer meant.

When she remained silent, thinking about the damage love could inflict, Sawyer said, "Not all relationships turn out like yours did, Jade."

He was treading on dangerous ground. He knew nothing about her relationship. Nothing. "I should hope not."

He stroked a finger down her arm and her breath caught in her throat. "I'm sorry."

It was the last thing she expected him to say. She softened, yearned.

Attracted and floundering, she searched for something mundane to say, though she couldn't take her eyes off his face. "Am I getting a sunburn?"

His mouth curved and a dimple erupted in one cheek. Her thoughts flew to kissing. Sawyer would be an expert.

"Sun-kissed." He tapped the end of her nose and winked. "Looks good on you."

Too close. Too appealing. Jade floundered for a snappy reply and found none. She could barely breathe.

Karen called from the awning. "Hey, you two. Burgers are ready when you are."

"Be right there." Sawyer waved a lazy hand but his gaze remained fixed on Jade.

She squirmed a little but didn't back away. Some powerful electric current seemed to freeze them in place. Hunger forgotten, the only thing she really wanted to do was lean into his strong chest and feel his arms around her.

She was one messed-up chick.

Sawyer's lips moved. "Ready?"

She certainly was.

He unwound his long length and bounced to a stand. For a moment, Jade felt disoriented. Then Sawyer reached a hand toward her. She accepted his strong carpenter's grip, and let him pull her up. He did so easily, as if she weighed nothing at all.

When he didn't let go, she didn't protest, didn't pull away. Perhaps she should have but she didn't. They walked together, Sawyer chatting in his easy way about his father's perfect burgers and his personal disdain for dill pickles.

Jade couldn't find her voice, so she let him talk. Her mind raced while her chest boiled with unwanted emotions. He was a client. She shouldn't hold his hand. He was a womanizer. She should run the other way.

None of those arguments made a bit of difference.

If any of the Buchanons noticed the hand-holding episode, they said nothing. When he let go, she felt the loss. Foolish woman that she was.

Somehow she managed to put together a hamburger, though she was acutely aware of Sawyer's nearness as he reached across her for mayo.

"You know, I've been thinking." Dan squirted mustard on a burger patty. "We haven't had any break-ins since Jade came on the job."

Karen, balancing a paper plate on her lap, said, "Then we better keep her around."

Sawyer's eyes captured hers, serious for once. "Yes," he said. "I think we better."

Chapter Eight

❧

"You better come outside."

Sawyer was barely out of bed and still half-asleep, but from the grim expression on Dawson's face, he'd better wake up fast. His brother showed up on his stoop fairly often, considering they lived side by side, but this was different. A difference Sawyer suspected he wasn't going to like.

"What's wrong?" He chugged a long drink of Coke. The burn snapped him into focus. His eyes watered.

"You're gonna hate this." His twin pivoted on his blue athletic shoes and walked away.

Growing more alarmed with every step his brother took, Sawyer put the Coke can back inside and followed Dawson across the small lawn to the driveway where he'd left his truck parked last night. Halfway there, he stopped, squinted, barely believing his eyes.

"No way." A sick dread gripped his gut.

"The other side is worse."

Sawyer emitted a pained groan.

Sprayed in garish orange paint across the full length of his beautiful maroon truck were the words, "You'll be sorry."

He thought he might lose his soda right here on the front lawn. "Sorry for what? What did I do?"

"So much for our vandal backing off."

His head snapped around to stare at Dawson. "You think this is the same person?"

"Don't you? Surely we don't have that many enemies."

"Yeah. Yeah. Must be." Sawyer tilted his head back and stared straight up. The blue June sky didn't cheer him one bit. "What's on the other side?"

"Something you're going to want to cover fast." They walked around together.

Sawyer's body sagged at the desecration. Along with a collection of disturbing obscenities, someone had scrawled the word "Cheater."

"So, Dad's right. I am the focus of this nut."

"From the personal references? Most likely. Why'd you leave your pickup parked outside last night?"

After a long day at the lake, he'd dropped Jade and Bailey at the motel, come home and collapsed. The sun and water had wrecked him.

"I park in the drive half the time. This is Gabriel's Crossing." Safe, quiet, friendly. Neighbors helped neighbors.

"Better call Leroy and Jade."

Jade. She'd want to know.

He eyed the obscene graffiti. "I don't want her to read this."

"She's an investigator, Sawyer, a former cop. She's seen worse."

He perched both hands on his hips. "That doesn't mean it's a good thing. We Buchanons protect our women."

"'Our women'?" Dawson's look was mild but pointed. "I noticed you and Jade were pretty cozy yesterday. Am I missing something?"

"No, no. I was only—" Sawyer rubbed the back of his neck, perplexed. "Maybe."

"Hmpf."

That's all his brother said, but that was enough. For now.

His twin understood him as no one else did. Even when he didn't understand himself.

After a long, silent look passed between them, Dawson withdrew his cell phone and pushed one single number. Sadly, the police department was now on speed dial. While his brother explained the situation to the dispatcher, Sawyer growled in frustration and called Jade.

Before she arrived, he dressed, snapped photos of the damage and contacted the local body shop. He needed a paint job fast. Like, before Jade arrived.

Within thirty minutes' time, she came at him across his front lawn looking crisp, fresh and competent in a navy skirt and white top, her pale hair clipped up in some kind of mysteriously appealing glob at the back of her head.

The weirdest sense of relief came over him.

No greeting. No smile. No fond comments about the incredible time they'd had together yesterday— and it had been incredible. He'd gone to sleep with a happy face, a regular emoji man, aware that something positive was brewing between them.

"Show me." Today, Jade was all business, but Sawyer couldn't hide his grin. Her nose was sunburned, her cheeks kissed with pink.

"Can you take my word for it?" He'd moved the truck inside the garage out of sight. "The vocabulary is not…nice."

She cut him a no-nonsense glance. "Show me."

He'd known she would insist. Prickly PI. He poked at the remote and waited for the garage door hum to cease before leading the way inside.

Gentleman that he was, he took her to the driver's side first. She whipped a camera from her backpack and snapped a few shots.

"Did you see or hear anything?" she asked.

"I was dead to the world last night. Weren't you?"

"Yes." A pucker appeared in her brow. A pretty

pucker he was tempted to smooth away. "What do you suppose this means? Why should you, if you are indeed the target, be sorry? What have you done to rile someone to this extent?"

"I've asked myself those questions for days." He lifted his hands in helplessness. "Nada."

She moved around the truck. He followed, watching her reaction.

Her face tightened. "Ugly business."

"Sorry you had to see that."

"I'm a big girl."

"So you keep saying." He leaned an elbow on the fender. "Still not something a lady should have to read."

She snapped photos, looked at the graffiti from various angles, tested the paint with the tip of her finger. "Dry."

"Spray paint dries fast, especially in this heat."

"Have the police been informed?"

"Leroy will be here when he can. He was out on a domestic."

She paused. Her nostrils flared. Anger darkened her face. Quickly, she spun away.

Sawyer's frown deepened.

What was that about?

Domestic calls made Jade's blood boil. Her blood pressure rose at the very mention of some muscle-bound oaf knocking around a woman or kids.

Every cop instinct inside her wanted to take the call herself and toss the creep in jail. Permanently.

To work off the reaction, she rounded the truck several times and then moved out to the driveway and across the grass to look for evidence, careful not to usurp Leroy's role or disturb the crime scene.

Sawyer followed close behind. She felt him there, hovering, almost protective. The juxtaposition of the domestic call and Sawyer's concern that she shouldn't read swear words had her brain in a boggle.

"See anything?"

"Not yet." She took photos of the grass, the driveway, the street in front of his house.

He stood watching, hands on his hips, a distraction she couldn't afford. "Why are you doing that?"

"Later, I'll look at these enlarged. You never know what you might miss." When she'd finished in the front, she moved around to the side and then the back of the town house. What she saw stopped her in her tracks.

"Sawyer." She glanced over one shoulder and held a hand out behind her to stop his progress. "Don't come any farther. Someone's been back here. We want to preserve this."

His tanned skin paled. "Footprints?"

The impressions on the morning dew were light

but they led right up to his window. She back-tracked to where he stood.

"Someone walked through those woods—" she pointed "—across the edge of the golf course and looked in this back window."

His Adam's apple bobbed. "That's a guest bedroom. Mine's upstairs."

But his vandal didn't know that. Until last night.

This was personal. Very personal. Which meant his graffiti artist might be a woman. "Is there any chance you have a stalker?"

"A stalker? Seriously?" He scoffed, a short, disbelieving laugh. "No."

"No one? Nothing unusual? No girlfriend who won't turn you loose? No phone calls that hang up? No notes or emails or Facebook messages that make you uncomfortable or seem out of place?"

"No— I— Well…" His usually happy countenance darkened to midnight. He pulled a hand over his face. "I've had a couple of odd emails and a few weird Facebook messages, but that's social media for you. Everybody gets them. I didn't give them a second thought."

She offered her coldest, most professional glare. "How long have you gotten these?"

He shifted, clearly uncomfortable. "A while."

"A while? You've had possible evidence all along and you've been holding out on me?"

"No! Not intentionally anyway. I didn't think they were important."

She looked toward the sky and made a frustrated growling sound. "I'll want to see those. All of them."

"Okay. Sure thing."

She clenched her back teeth. "Now."

Now didn't happen immediately. Leroy arrived and took his report before they had a chance to retire inside the town house.

Sawyer knew Jade was miffed and the delay annoyed her to no end. She was as chilly as Denali in January.

After Leroy left, Sawyer phoned his parents to give them an update and announce regrets that he wouldn't make it to church this morning.

"Would you mind picking up Bailey and Ashton? I invited her but—" He let the rest dangle. Mom got it.

"Are you sure everything is safe at your house?" she asked.

He was admittedly a little freaked out. "Yeah. I'm fine. No worries. Jade is here and we're going over some ideas."

No way he would tell his mother about the weird emails until he knew if they were meaningful. Having one female upset with him was enough.

"Will you be here later for dinner?" Sunday afternoons were a tradition at the parents' house. He didn't like to miss it.

"Don't know." He eyed Jade. She paced like a

neat little lion around his living room, staring at everything as if he was hiding something. She was still fired up about the emails as if he'd intentionally kept them from her. "I'll ask Jade."

Jade's head whipped around, smoky eyes curious. His silly heart did a downbeat. He shot her a quick, if uncertain, smile, finished his conversation with Mom and rang off.

"Want something to drink?" His abandoned Coke had long gone flat. He ambled to the doorway between kitchen and living room. "Hot out there."

"Some water would be great."

"Got it." They'd come a long way. The first time she'd been in his house, she'd refused his offer of refreshment and dripped icicles all over the place. She wasn't really mad at him about the emails. She was worried.

Before he could get happy about that revelation, she appeared in the doorway. "Ask me what?"

"Are you eavesdropping on my convo with my mama?" He offered a smile so she'd know he joked, though he didn't figure she'd be amused.

"Hard not to." She crossed her arms but he detected a softening around that pretty mouth and a sparkle in her gray eyes. "Ask me what?"

"The Buchanons get together every Sunday morning for church and at Mom and Dad's house for food and fun in the afternoon. You're invited."

He twisted the top on a frosty water bottle and

handed it to her. Her fingers brushed his in the exchange and he had a flashback to the lake, holding hands, feeling a bit romancey.

"Thanks." She turned away with her drink, leaving him alone in the kitchen.

"'Thanks' isn't an answer." He popped the top on a fresh Coke and followed. "We had a great time yesterday, didn't we?"

"Yes. It was fantastic. Your family is very nice. The lake was perfect. I haven't enjoyed a day on the water in over a year." She actually smiled. "And your mad boating skills were impressive."

Would wonders never cease? She'd admitted what he already knew—she'd had a good time. And unless his radar had gone wonky, she liked him more than she wanted to admit, though he couldn't figure out why she resisted the idea. Was he that bad?

"You're a good skier," he said.

"So are you." Admittedly, he'd shown off to impress her when he'd had his turn on the water.

"We had fun together. You and me."

Her smile wavered. "We did. Thanks for taking me."

They stood staring at each other while some emotion pinged through the atmosphere. She'd accused him of holding back, but she was holding back, as well.

Divorce, he supposed, could do that to you. Distrust. Uncertainty. Lumping all guys into the same category. Was that the problem?

"So what do you say? Later this afternoon with the Buchanon clan?"

"Maybe. If I have time." She motioned toward his laptop. "Now let's see those posts and emails."

Sawyer sipped his soda and ambled to the couch.

He could be content with maybe.

Jade settled on the sofa next to Sawyer and his laptop. He smelled clean, like soap and water, though he hadn't shaved today. No time, she supposed, after discovering the graffiti on his truck. Not that she was complaining. The scruff only added to his tanned good looks.

"I deleted the emails but they should still be in my trash folder." He scrolled through the long list, and if he was bothered by having her look over his shoulder and pry into his personal email account, he didn't let on.

"Here. This one." He clicked on an email and she leaned in to read the rambling love letter. With her side touching his and his breath on her cheek, she struggled to focus on the email. All she had to do was turn her head and there he was, scruffy beard, blue eyes and manly face.

She cleared her throat and stared at the computer screen, too aware of him. "You have a secret admirer."

She wasn't surprised by that. Probably lots of girls crushed on him and never let on. But had this particular one taken her feelings too far and become a stalker?

Sawyer was shaking his head. "I don't buy the secret admirer idea. Buchanons shoot from the hip, straight and honest."

Did they? Really? She wondered what her father would say to that.

"You may be an upfront kind of person. That doesn't mean she is." Jade ran her gaze over the letter a second time.

"She calls herself 'your special girl.' Doesn't that bring anyone to mind? Some girl you've given a pet name to? Some secret love you don't want your family to know about?"

She lifted her eyes and they were face-to-face, way too close. Not close enough.

Her heart did a painful rhythm. She battled to remember that Sawyer was a client and she was on the job.

Sawyer was clearly oblivious to the turmoil going on inside her. He flicked a glance in her direction and then back to the screen, all business. Which she should be.

"I told you. I'm not fond of secrets. Not that kind anyway. I don't date anyone my family wouldn't approve of."

Had his family approved of her?

She pushed that aberrant thought back into hiding. He didn't like secrets and she had plenty he didn't know about.

"You require your family's approval to date a woman? That sounds a bit archaic."

"I don't *require* anything. I want their approval."

Were the Buchanons controlling? Demanding? Forceful and judgmental when he didn't bow to their expectations? Like her father. "Family first?"

"Nope. God comes first. Family second."

The God issue again. "Will you be ostracized if you don't abide by their beliefs?"

He gave her the strangest look. "Seriously? Does my family seem that way to you?"

No, they didn't. They'd been warm and receptive and genuinely interested in her. They'd even gone to the trouble of bringing homemade oatmeal cookies because they'd somehow discovered those were her favorite.

"I'm trying to get a clearer picture of your family dynamics." True enough, but not because of the case.

"We're as transparent as they come, Jade. Plain and simple, we love and respect each other. We like to be together. We like serving God and our community as a family unit. It's the Buchanon way."

The Buchanon way sounded nothing like the Clifton way. Was their idea of Christian faith different, too?

Flummoxed, she turned to the screen and pointed. "Email this to me. I'll try to trace the source."

He gave her a strange look but didn't press. Instead, he followed her directions to forward the email. His fingers moved quickly over the keyboard, competent, as he seemed to be in so many things.

Fighting to remain professional, she said, "Let's have a look at the Facebook messages."

He logged in to his profile page, his shoulder rubbing against hers as he typed.

After their day at the lake, she'd lain awake in the motel for hours, reliving every moment, remembering the feel of her hand in his, the flash of his smile, the concern he'd shown on the water. He wasn't what she'd expected, a truth that messed with her head.

That he was handsome was a given, but more than looks fueled Sawyer's appeal. Was he for real? Was all this familial love and harmony on the up-and-up?

She watched his hands, strong and masculine, working the keys. He was, she knew, left-hand dominant, and a long scar ran between his thumb and forefinger.

"I didn't notice that yesterday."

"What?" He stopped typing.

"The scar." Without a second thought, she reached out and traced it with her index finger.

His skin was firm and very warm. An unbidden zip arced up her arm.

Sawyer shifted slightly toward her. Had he felt it, too?

He turned his hand over, wrapped her fingers with his.

His expression had gone serious, searching.

Jade swallowed. She shouldn't have touched him. They were already too cozy, particularly since she couldn't stop thinking about yesterday. About him.

His gaze fell to her lips. He wanted to kiss her. And she wanted him to.

Was she so programmed to fall for the wrong men that she couldn't help herself?

She jerked her hand from his, swallowed thickly and moved toward the coffee table, ostensibly to retrieve her notebook but mostly to regain her equilibrium.

He'd given her more than a potential stalker to think about. A lot more.

Chapter Nine

Friday evening after work, Dawson dropped Sawyer at the body shop for his newly painted truck. His ride looked sweet again, shiny and unmarred by the obscenities he still wished Jade hadn't seen.

Thoughts of Jade were never far away. He was getting in deep with a woman who kept him at arm's length. Most of the time.

One minute Sawyer thought they had something going, and the next she was as cold as the tundra. In spite of everything, he liked her. He'd seen beneath the chilly detective's mask to the woman. She was smart and athletic, she knew how to play and her concern for Bailey and Ashton spoke volumes about her character. There was a good person under that stiff detective exterior.

Something more than this case troubled her, though. He was praying about it, about her. For her.

He regretted the near kiss, and not only because

it hadn't happened, though he definitely regretted that part. Worse, their sparks had ignited her reserve and she'd backed out on the afternoon with him and his family.

He'd been bummed enough to talk to Dawson about her, about the way she blew hot and cold, about his own growing desire to be more than her investigation. His twin advised him to give her time and space. If something was there, she'd come around.

In the week since the graffiti incident, he had taken his brother's advice and kept things light and easy even though he'd been with her every day, a necessity for digging into his life, his friends, his college days, his work relationships. No stone was left unturned. As uncomfortable as the invasion of privacy was, he enjoyed the time with Jade.

The fact that he used the case as an excuse to buy her lunch, and as often as he could her dinner, which sometimes turned into long walks by the river—to discuss the case, of course—didn't shame him one bit. He hadn't even held her hand.

Focusing on the more important matter of faith, he had invited her to church, which led to a conversation about his personal relationship with Christ. This time she listened, asking questions in her astute detective manner. She'd said little and he didn't know where she stood, but she was thawing.

Like Dawson, Mom said she'd been hurt and

that he should tread easy, both as an interested man and as a Christian. Living faith was a more powerful witness than talking about it.

He didn't figure he could tread any easier. If Jade didn't know he was a good guy by now, would she ever?

He cranked the truck engine, listened with pleasure at the diesel rumble and prepared to drive away. His cell phone buzzed against his hip. He left the vehicle in Park and answered.

"Sawyer here. Who's this?"

"Sawyer? This is Kinley. Something kind of weird happened today."

Kinley Aimes. They'd dated off and on last year. Gorgeous brunette who could dance like a pro. Nice girl. "Something weird? Are you okay?"

"I'm good, but I thought you should know a woman stopped by my work. She was asking questions about you."

The hair at the back of his neck tingled. Jade thought he had a stalker. Was his stalker now after his former girlfriends?

"Did you get a name?"

"She said she was a private investigator working on a case for your family. But her questions seemed off. She made me uncomfortable."

Jade? Why would she be talking to Kinley? Had he even given her Kinley's name? "Off? Like how?"

"She asked about us, about when we were seeing each other. I thought it was a strange conversation."

Oh. That made sense. Part of the investigation. Maybe she was ruling out stalkers. Not that he would enlighten Kinley on that front.

"Nothing to worry about, Kin. She's working for my dad, investigating vandalism to Buchanon Built properties."

"I've heard about that. But why is she asking about you? And why is she getting so personal?"

The word penetrated his thick skull. "Personal? How personal?"

"She didn't ask much about me or about the vandalism. She wanted to know about your temper."

"Me? A temper?"

Kinley laughed. "That's what I told her. You're the least tempestuous guy I know, but she was a little pushy and insisted on asking about your behavior. Were you the jealous type? Did you control where I went or who my friends were? Did you get upset if I talked to other guys? Had you ever hit me?"

Sawyer gripped the cell phone in a stranglehold. "She asked you that? For real?"

"Yes. It was a really strange moment, Sawyer. I'm sorry. I thought you should know someone is saying this kind of thing about you."

Somehow he managed to finish the conversation with the appropriate assurances and thanks.

As he pressed End, he stared out at the busy street, seeing nothing but trouble.

He didn't have a temper. He wasn't mean or abusive. But right now, he was running between bewildered and steamed.

He and Nancy Drew had some serious talking to do.

Jade sat cross-legged on the motel bed, computer on her lap and notes at her side. Her brain was exhausted and she needed a break but she'd learned some interesting things today. Some of which she should share with Sawyer. Some. Definitely not all.

She reached for her cell. He'd been different this week, careful, almost solicitous. He'd kept a friendly distance. Oh, he'd been Mr. Charm and Smiles, but he hadn't been the least romantic. He hadn't even held her hand. Not once.

Which was great. Fine. Dandy. Friendly and businesslike was for the best.

Even if it left her a little miserable and lonely at the end of each day. Especially on the evenings he or someone in his family swept Bailey and Ashton away for dinner or some church event. They invited her, too, but she always declined.

Jade rubbed her eyes and stretched. Why had she said no? Was she that afraid?

A knock sounded on her door. "Hey, Nancy. You in there?"

Her heart leaped like a circus flea. Sawyer.

She padded on bare feet to the door. "Who's there?"

"The Big Bad Wolf. Open up before I blow your house down."

She opened up.

He didn't smile. "We need to talk."

"I'm busy—"

"Now works for me."

Before she could react, he barged into her room and shut the door behind him. Mr. Charm wasn't happy. He bordered on anger. Maybe worse.

A breath caught in Jade's throat. She backed up a few steps and bumped into the built-in desk.

They were alone. She had nowhere to run. He was bigger, more muscular. And he'd caught her off guard.

Self-defense training floated through her mind. If he raised a hand, she'd fight back. She wouldn't be a victim again. She would not cower.

With much effort, she forced herself to straighten and clench her fists. Ready.

Sawyer tilted his head. His expression went from anger to confusion. "What's wrong with you? Why are you looking at me like that?"

She licked dry lips. "Like what?"

"Scared." Light dawned on his face. "Did you learn something? Did someone threaten you?"

He moved then and she let him, aware she was overreacting.

"No." To regain her composure, she turned her back, pretending to look through a folder on the desk. When she thought she had herself together, she whipped around, pasting on a pleasant expression. "What did you want to talk to me about?"

"Are you sure you're okay? You look—"

"I'm fine. Now what do you want?" There. Crisp. Professional. To the point.

If only she wasn't dressed in yoga pants and flip-flops.

He gave her a once-over, as if he still thought she had a screw loose, but settled with saying, "You paid a visit to a friend of mine today. Kinley."

How did he know that?

"I did. And to several other girls whose names you gave me." She reached behind and drew out the folder. "I have them all in here."

"Must be crowded."

She blinked, bewildered for a second before the joke settled in. "Oh. Funny."

"You don't look amused. And I'm not, either. Why are you bothering my friends with this? None of them would vandalize my truck."

"I can't leave any stone unturned, Sawyer. Even though you believe the best about your friends, people sometimes hide who they really are." She flipped open the folder. "Like your stalker friend. Her email is fake. So is her Facebook and other social media files."

"Is that so?"

"She uses a fake name, photos of lesser-known actresses as her profile pics and leaves no useful identifying information."

His frown deepened to a scowl. "Why would anyone do that?"

She shrugged. "A number of reasons. Privacy. Safety."

"Or to cover her tracks."

"If our perp is female."

"What if it's a man using this as a ploy to throw us off?"

The idea scared her to pieces. "Possible but doubtful. I see desperation, maybe unrequited love, feelings of rejection."

"That's stupid."

"There are a lot of women's names in my file."

"Friends."

"That's what I hear." Every last female she'd called or visited claimed she and Sawyer remained friends after they stopped dating. Did anyone really do that? Or were they covering up for him? For themselves?

"If you'd bother to ask, I have male friends, too." He pivoted to her fridge. "Got any Cokes in here?"

"No."

He huffed a weary, put-upon breath and crossed his arms. "All right, then. I need to know something. And I expect a straight answer."

She didn't like the look in his eyes.

"Why did you ask Kinley if I'd ever hit her? What's that got to do with someone spray painting my truck?"

Jade imitated his posture and crossed her arms. "Procedure."

"No." His head wagged from side to side. "I don't buy that. Something else is going on here."

"I spoke with five women today and asked them all the same questions." Unable to hold his gaze any longer, she dropped her stance and pretended to rummage through the file.

She felt him move across the motel room, felt his size and height in the small space. Though the hair rose on the back of her neck, she didn't turn around, didn't cower. If Sawyer's women spoke the truth, she had nothing to fear.

A strong hand touched her shoulder.

In spite of everything, she flinched.

"Why do you do that?" His voice had grown soft and was a breath away from her ear. His new-wood scent whispered around her like his voice.

She gulped. "Do what?"

The murmured words trembled.

"Jade." Slowly, he turned her around and took the clutched file from her death grip. "All these questions today about my temper and violence. Then tonight you jump as if you're afraid of me. If someone said I hurt them, they lied and I need to know."

She was already shaking her head. "No one."

"Then what's going on? I thought we liked each other. I'm not the grim reaper."

She forced a laugh. "I know that."

"Let's get something straight." His piercing gaze never left her face. "I don't hit women. Ever. I don't push them or slap them or force them to do anything they don't want to. And I'm offended that you would think that."

"I don't." She didn't. She really didn't. But the defense mechanisms had become second nature.

"Yes, you do. Or maybe it's not me. Maybe it was the jerk you divorced."

She went very still, barely breathing. Talking about the abuse made her vulnerable. She couldn't appear vulnerable to a client.

She turned her head to one side, away from his intensely interested gaze. If her heart beat any faster, she'd need a defibrillator. Paddles to the chest. Electroshock.

As gentle as a breath, Sawyer touched her chin and tugged her back to face him. "I said the magic words, didn't I? The ex."

She remained silent but tears prickled the back of her eyelids. She did not cry. She would not cry. Crying was a weak woman's weapon.

But Sawyer, with his gift for people, saw what she tried to hide. The expression on his face changed, melting her. Compassion, devastation.

Her family had blamed her. She'd provoked

Cam. She was stubborn, uncooperative, a bad wife. She got what she deserved.

"I'm right, aren't I?" His voice was so tender and understanding, she nodded.

His arms came around her immediately. He drew her to his chest, lightly, carefully.

"Oh, Jade. Sweetheart. I'm sorry." Long fingers caressed her hair, smoothing it over and over again as he had his niece when she'd scraped a knee at the lake. Gentle, protective, caring.

Letting down six years of carefully erected guard, she laid her head against his thudding, thudding heart and rested.

Sawyer was a peaceful man. He normally made friends, not foes. Somewhere along the line, he'd made a powerful enemy who vandalized his family's property. And now he had another. A man he didn't know. A man he'd like to get his hands on for five long minutes in a private setting. Man-to-man.

Carpentry had made him strong. He could do some serious damage if he wanted to. Right now, he wanted to.

As tenderly as knew how, he held Jade against him and stroked her hair, her back, and if he kissed the top of her head, he wasn't sorry. She needed comfort. She tried to put on a brave front, but she was wounded.

"Want to tell me about it?"

At first she shook her head no, so he didn't press. He simply held her. She made no attempt to move and seemed perfectly content where she was. So was he. Holding Jade was something he'd thought about often but he'd been waiting for the right moment.

He'd had something decidedly more romantic in mind. But for now, she needed him, and that was enough.

The room grew quiet until the only sounds were their mingled breaths and the outside noises. Cars passed in a hiss on hot pavement. A heavy unit door slammed nearby. Vague voices drifted through the paper-thin walls of the old motel.

Then she began to speak. Softly at first, almost as if to herself. She told of Cam, her husband of three years. Three years with a man who alternated between sweetness and gifts to control and anger. He'd bought her a new Mercedes the day after he'd knocked out a tooth.

"He promised it would never happen again."

He could feel her trembling. Even remembering the abuse was traumatic. "And you wanted to believe him."

"If I would try harder, it wouldn't happen. If I wouldn't make him angry. If I could be the good wife he expected me to be." Her words grew stronger, more defiant. "We were married two years before I realized the problem was him instead of my inadequacies."

"Why didn't you leave then?"

She pulled away from his embrace and crossed her arms again. Then, as if she realized she didn't need a defensive posture with him, she let her arms fall to her sides.

"Women keep silent. Submit to your husbands. A divorced woman is an adulteress, a Jezebel. I've had those scriptures forced down my throat since I was a child." She made a scoffing sound that pricked his heart. "My father insists I'm doomed for all eternity unless I return to Cam."

Somebody's theology was seriously twisted. "That's wrong, Jade. Those scriptures are in the Bible, sure, but the context is off."

She tossed her head. "Whatever. I don't really care anymore. I'm rid of Cam and religion."

"Good for you for tossing Cam. But don't throw Jesus out with the bathwater."

She backed away, face tight. "Don't preach to me, Sawyer. I've had enough of that to last a lifetime."

He raised both hands. "No preaching. Just remember that real men don't have to force their women to do anything. They sure don't hit them. Real men take care of women."

"I can take care of myself." She crossed her arms again, tight as shrink-wrap.

"You shouldn't have to. Not alone. The Bible says two are better than one because if one falls down, the other can help them up." He stretched a hand toward her. "Let me help you up, Jade."

"I'm the investigator. I'm supposed to be helping you."

He kept his hand extended, waiting, his chest hot with compassion and yearning. "We can help each other."

A dozen emotions flickered across her face until at last she softened. Slowly, she extended her hand and with her gaze pinned to his, reading him, making sure she could trust his motives, she moved back into his embrace.

Sawyer felt as if he'd conquered Mount Everest.

Chapter Ten

Sunday morning, Jade stood in front of the wavy motel mirror with a curling iron and a hairbrush. Somehow Sawyer, with help from Bailey, had persuaded her to attend church as a prelude to dinner at his parents' home.

The very idea formed a knot in her stomach so tight she'd need Houdini to untie it.

She enjoyed the Buchanons, having spent every day with at least one of them. And the lake trip had been terrific. The big noisy family was all right, cordial, even likable. But church? What had she been thinking to willingly subject herself to fire and brimstone so hot it singed her hair? Hadn't she had enough of that growing up?

Sawyer Buchanon was getting to her. That's all there was to it.

Check that. Sawyer had gotten to her. With his warmth and charm, he'd tunneled through her barriers and made her like him. Not that she fully trusted him, but she felt something she'd never felt before, not even for Cam in their early days before she learned of the monster hidden behind the smile and a bouquet of roses.

People, she'd learned the hard way, were not always who they presented to the rest of the world. Sawyer seemed like the real deal, but she wasn't foolish. He might be hiding something, the way he'd hidden the secret admirer emails. Sure, he denied he was hiding them, but she couldn't be positive.

Emotions would never rule her life again.

The curling iron clattered against the desktop. She turned it off. Should she go or not?

Long after Sawyer had left the other night Jade had pondered their conversation, a talk that had lasted into the late hours. She was still amazed that she'd told him about Cam. Not everything, of course. Some hurts cut too deep.

The fact that he'd tiptoed around her aversion to his faith, all the while displaying his in the gentlest way, didn't escape notice.

She wasn't stupid. She knew there were different kinds of Christians. The trouble was she'd blocked all mention of God out of her life after escaping Cam and Southview.

And then Sawyer came along.

Caution lights flashed like red and yellow fireworks inside her head.

Bailey would be disappointed if she backed out now.

"Bailey will be fine." She had friends at the Lighthouse Church and a nursery full of workers with tons of baby toys for Ashton.

She leaned into the funhouse mirror and stroked mascara onto her lashes.

Church was only a couple of hours. She could endure it. And Sawyer was probably already on his way.

But why should she have to?

Why indeed?

With a click, she recapped the mascara and went for her cell phone. In seconds, Sawyer was on the line. She opened her mouth to tell a lie when someone pecked on the door.

"Jade?" Bailey's voice came through the flimsy wood loud and clear.

"Just a second, Sawyer." Jade spoke into the receiver. "Bailey's outside."

She crossed the small space and opened the door.

"You don't look ready for church." In fact, Bailey looked exhausted and scared. "Is something wrong?"

Bailey nodded and burst into tears.

Instinctively, Jade pulled the young mom and her baby into her room, stepped out and scanned the area.

A tinny voice inside her cell phone said, "Jade.

Is Bailey all right? What's wrong? I hear her crying. What's going on?"

Ashton whimpered, drowning out the rest of Sawyer's words.

Satisfied that the area was clear, Jade closed the door and shoved the dead bolt, before speaking to Sawyer. "I'll call you back."

Before he could argue, she pushed End and tossed the phone toward the unmade bed.

She guided the sobbing teenager to a corner of the bed and sat down beside her. "Talk to me. Did someone hurt you? Did someone break in? Are you sick?"

"Ashton."

Jade noticed what she hadn't before. A listless Ashton lay against Bailey's chest, his face flushed, his eyes glassy.

Jade placed a hand on his little forehead. "He's burning up."

Bailey nodded, tears streaking her young face. "I don't know what to do. He's never been sick."

"Did you take his temperature?"

"I don't have a thermometer." And she burst into fresh tears. "I'm scared, Jade. I'm a horrible mother. I don't know how to do this. He won't eat and he just lays there like he's dying. Is he going to die, Jade?"

Jade's years of cop training clicked in. Brusquely, with forced confidence, she replied, "Of course not. Babies get fevers easily."

She had no idea if that was true.

"He was fussy last night but when he finally stopped crying, I went to sleep, thinking he was okay. But he's not. He's not okay." Bailey's face contorted. "I'm a terrible mom. I should have stayed awake. He needed me and I was asleep! What if he had died?"

Jade put her arm around the distraught girl. She was exhausted, scared and too young to handle a baby alone. Jade didn't know a lot about babies either, and her first responder training didn't cover fevers.

"Let's calm down. Okay? He will be fine, but Ashton needs you to have a clear head right now." She kept her voice kind but firm and confident. "Deep breath. Blow it out."

Bailey shuddered in a chest full of air but sobbed on the exhale.

Carefully, Jade lifted the hot baby from his mother's arms. He felt limp and lifeless. Her adrenaline jacked a notch higher.

"We'll take him to the emergency room and get him checked out. Okay?"

Bailey nodded, wiping at her face with the backs of her hands.

"Tissue in the bathroom. Splash some water on your face too and we'll go." She didn't even know where the nearest hospital was but GPS would get her there.

The door to her unit shook under a pounding fist. "Jade. It's Sawyer. Let me in."

A familiar voice. Someone who knew the town and doctors. Thank goodness.

Baby in one arm, she slid the dead bolt. Handsome in slacks, shirt and tie, a harried Sawyer plunged inside. He took one look at Ashton and said, "He's sick."

Fighting the instant attraction, Jade snarled. "You don't have to be a detective to know that."

If Sawyer was insulted, he didn't let on, and she instantly felt like a jerk for barking at him.

"Hey, little man. What's wrong, buddy?" Sawyer placed a hand on Ashton's forehead. Worried blue eyes flickered up to hers. "He's burning up."

Grimly, she nodded. "We're headed to the ER."

Tissue pressed against her nose, Bailey exited the bathroom, spotted Sawyer and burst into fresh sobs. He crossed the room and folded her into his arms.

"Hey, we got this, little sis. We got this." He rocked her back and forth for a minute while Jade's insides turned over and her heart squeezed.

He released Bailey, dazzled her with a reassuring smile and guided her toward the door. "Get in my truck. I'll take you. We'll have this little guy fixed up in time for Sunday dinner."

Jade didn't argue. The baby was the important thing here, not her rather significant relief at discovering Sawyer Buchanon outside her door.

* * *

The Gabriel's Crossing Hospital sprawled on the south edge of town, three blocks from the fire station and fifteen minutes from the River Roost Motel. Sawyer drove there in ten.

Babies, he assured Bailey on the short drive, spiked fevers over the simplest thing. Ashton probably had a cold. He'd conjured up all the calming things he'd heard his mother say to his sister when Ryan and Amber were babies.

Still, turning the teen and her baby over to Gena Satterfield, nurse practitioner, brought instant relief. Gena was a first-rate pro and practically family. She'd take good care of Ashton.

The nurse whisked Mom and baby away with her usual efficient cheer and left him and Jade to wait.

He sat next to Jade in a green vinyl chair, hands clasped between his knees, eyes shut as he prayed for Ashton to be okay.

"Bailey's too young to handle this alone."

Sawyer swiveled his head toward Jade. "She's not alone. She has us."

"For today. But what about the next time? What about the rest of her life?"

Her knuckles had gone white where she squeezed the chair arm. The episode had shaken her. Not so much, he thought, because of the sick baby but because Bailey lived alone, without family support. Like Jade, apparently.

"One thing at a time, okay?" He took the liberty of placing his hand atop hers. Even though the temperature outside was hot, her fingers were cold. "Let's get Ashton well. We'll figure out the rest from there."

He'd expected her to argue but instead, she chewed that intriguing bottom lip and momentarily took his mind off Ashton.

We, he'd said. As if Jade would be around to help. That she wouldn't be soured his stomach.

He tapped a message into his phone. His family would add Ashton to today's prayer requests.

"You're missing church again," Jade said.

"Jesus knows where I am. He was always more concerned about people's needs than a church building anyway."

She gave him a funny look and he understood. His faith didn't match her distorted view of God. He was praying for her. Had the whole family on their knees.

Admittedly, his heart had gone a little *bonk-bonk* when Jade opened the door with a baby in her arms. She'd looked soft and motherly, though soft wasn't a word Jade wanted anyone to use in her regard. She tried so hard to be tough.

He understood that, too, now that he knew about the ex-husband. If Sawyer ever met Cam Warren, they'd both need prayer.

He stretched out his long legs to get more comfortable and brought Jade's hand to rest on his knee, holding her there.

A man entered the emergency room, a towel held to his hand. A brunette woman followed, red purse under one arm.

"Chet?" Sawyer sat up straight, releasing Jade's hand. "What happened? Are you okay?"

"Aw, nothing serious. A little cut." Chet hitched a chin toward the woman now at the reception desk. "Livy thinks I need stitches."

Livy, a robust woman in glasses and sneakers, turned her head. "And a tetanus shot. Hiya, Sawyer."

"Livy." He offered a courteous nod. "Anything I can do?"

"Short of taking away his power tools? Not a thing." She shook her head as though disgusted with the whole male gender.

The two men exchanged amused glances before a scrub-clad nurse stepped out to take the couple back to an exam room.

The ER was slow this Sunday morning. Thankfully.

"Do you know everyone in Gabriel's Crossing?" Jade reached for one of the dog-eared, battered magazines lying on an end table.

"Mostly. The blessing of a small town."

"Or the curse. You likely know your stalker. Maybe see her every day."

His stomach clenched. The stalker hadn't been

on his mind—until now. *Thanks a lot, Jade.* "Disturbing thought."

His cell phone buzzed. Sawyer looked down. "From Dawson. The family had prayer for Ashton. Wants to know if they should come down here."

"Why would they do that?"

"The Buchanon way. Doesn't your family come running when you need them?"

Her jaw tightened. "I'm an adult. I don't need them to come running."

The adamant response convinced him all was not well with her family. He couldn't imagine. "You're not close?"

"Close enough."

She turned prickly again and he knew he'd stepped on troubled territory. She had brothers. She'd shared that much, and they'd once skied together. But not in a long time.

Something had happened.

"I wouldn't want to be without my family around. They're awesome people."

"Not everyone has that, Sawyer."

"I'm sorry."

"Me, too." Her bottom lip quivered, vulnerable. She turned her head away.

Sawyer wanted badly to comfort her. Jade could seem alone in a crowded room. He wanted to wrap her in his arms the way he had at the motel last week. To feel her heartbeat against his, her breath against his neck.

She pricked his heart, and he was still trying to wrap his head around the way she made him feel.

His phone chimed again. He read the message. "They'll wait dinner for us."

"They don't have to do that."

"But they will." His thumbs moved over the keyboard. "I told him we'd let them know as soon as Gena comes out with news about Ashton."

She went back to her magazine, though he could tell from the way she flipped pages that her mind was elsewhere.

Time ticked past, marked by the commercials on Sunday-morning television programs.

He spotted them before Jade did and an inner smile moved to his lips.

"What are you smiling about?"

He hadn't known she was watching.

He pointed toward the glass doors.

Jade's face grew incredulous as the parade of Buchanons streamed into the waiting area. His parents, his brothers and sisters. Even Brady and Abby, back only one or two days from their honeymoon, were here.

He'd known they would come. No amount of reassurance would keep them away.

Sawyer stood, aware of how blessed he was to have this giant bunch of people who loved him. No matter his failures and quirks, they were there for him. Bailey didn't have that kind of support. Neither did Jade.

"Any news yet?" His mother came straight to him for a hug. She smelled like summer flowers, familiar and cheering.

"No, but Gena's got him."

Quinn nodded, pride shining on his face as vivid as Abby and Brady's Italian glow. "Best doc in town, even if she's a nurse."

Jade looked from one Buchanon to the other, apparently stunned by the overwhelming support. "But you were at church…"

"We spoke to Pastor and asked for prayer before leaving. He understands family emergencies."

Mom's statement seemed to confuse Jade even more. "Ashton and Bailey aren't your family."

"Family of God. They need us. We're here." Dawson flopped into one of the green chairs, long legs identical to his twin's in navy dress slacks. The rest of the family scattered around the small waiting area, taking up all the vacant seats.

The quiet waiting room was suddenly less cold and anesthetic.

Sawyer and Jade filled in the details they knew about Ashton's illness, and then they settled in to wait, chatting about this and that, mostly about Brady's honeymoon. Anything to pass the time.

Dad, with his usual workaholic energy, paced the room and stared out the window a few times.

Brady and Abby snuggled together on a love seat to exchange loving looks and to share honeymoon photos with Charity and Jaylee.

"Want to see these, Jade?" Jaylee patted the corner of her chair. His youngest sister was so thin, petite Jade easily fit in the extra space.

The distraction, Sawyer thought, was good for her. And he enjoyed watching her with his family.

By the time Gena finally ushered Bailey and Ashton to the waiting room, the nurse practitioner was smiling. Bailey looked less frightened.

Sawyer stood. The rest of the Buchanons rose with him, a wall of protection and support. "What's the verdict?"

"Ear infection." Gena held a prescription in one hand. "Baby fever reducer and antibiotics should fix him up. He'll probably sleep most of the day." She settled a steady look at Bailey. "And his mother should do the same."

Sawyer reached for the Rx. The tension in his shoulders eased.

"I'll take that." He winked at Bailey. "Your hands are full."

His mama, God bless her, slipped an arm around the teenager. "You're coming home with us, honey. We'll look after Ashton so you can get some rest. After you have a good dinner."

"Oh, I couldn't."

"Why not?"

"I—" The yearning on the girl's face was undeniable.

"Don't argue with Mom." Sawyer shot Bailey

an easy, encouraging smile and a quick wink. "She always wins."

The Buchanon women flanked the young mother. Charity lifted the baby from her arms and laid him over one shoulder to pat his little back. "Both of you need rest and we're all at Mom's house today anyway. We'd love to watch this little prince while you catch a nap."

At times like this, he adored his big sister.

"Trust me, I know how crucial sleep can be when you have a sick child." This from Abby, who'd weathered many illnesses alone with her special needs daughter until she'd met Brady and been enveloped by the Buchanon clan.

"I *am* really tired," Bailey admitted. "But Jade—"

"Jade's coming, too." Sawyer knew an advantage when he had one. Jade wouldn't let Bailey down.

Bailey nodded, relief hanging on her like a robe. "Okay, then. Thanks."

Before Jade could utter a word of protest, Sawyer took her elbow and ushered her to his truck.

Who were these people? Were they for real?

Sunday afternoon at the Buchanon home was like nothing Jade had ever experienced. Even the few friends who had invited her to their homes as a teenager didn't have families like this one.

The sprawling split-level home on Barley Street

rocked with laughter and conversation. The smell of bacon-wrapped chicken from Dan's patio smoker had everyone salivating and groaning while they waited for side dishes to be completed.

Feeling at loose ends, Jade hung around the long bar separating a huge kitchen from an even bigger family/dining room. With seven kids, she supposed the enormous space and the long, banquet-style table were warranted.

Bailey, too exhausted to wait for dinner, had been put to bed in something called "the apartment" off the garage. Apparently, Abby and Lila had lived there for a while when their house was being built and in the subsequent days after the fire destroyed the new home Brady had built for her.

As soon as the girl and baby were settled, the Buchanons formed a huddle in the family room. Jade stood on the perimeter, curious as she listened to a discussion of Bailey's situation.

They expressed concern and tossed around ideas. Not once did she hear anyone malign the teenager for being an unwed mother. No one spouted dire scriptures about her sinfulness. No one condemned her to punishment and misery.

Allison, sitting next to her husband, Jake, bracketed her baby bump. "I can't imagine being alone with my baby, no support, no family to call in times of stress."

"Social services can only do so much." Quinn massaged his damaged shoulder.

"No social service can offer love and a promise to be available anytime, anywhere."

"But we can." Karen looped an arm with her husband's. "We're in the perfect position to give it. Aren't we, Dan?"

The older Buchanons made a handsome couple. Tall and dark like his sons, Dan's slight paunch didn't detract from his looks and blonde, middle-aged Karen was beautiful.

It wasn't their looks, though, that intrigued Jade. It was the way Dan treated Karen with respect and admiration, as an equal, instead of like a brainless doormat. And Karen clearly admired her husband. They formed a team, banded together for a common goal.

Nothing like her parents, for sure.

"Another rug rat around here is exactly what this big old house needs." Dan's expression grew tender as he gazed from Karen to little Lila pushing her walker around the patio outside. "We're going to miss our Princess Lila around here."

Brady laughed. "She won't be that far away, Dad."

"Still gonna miss hearing her giggles."

"Yes, we are." Karen patted Dan's arm. "So the issue of Bailey and Ashton is settled. We'll ask them to move in with us while she finishes school and gets on her feet."

Jade blinked at Karen's statement. While she finished school? That was more than an afternoon of kindness. That was long-term. "You'd do that?"

"Welcome to the Buchanon menagerie, Jade." Sawyer's smile spoke of his familial pride. If the Buchanons were for real, he had a right to be.

Dan clapped his hands once, as if that finalized everything. "Now that we have that settled, who's hungry?"

Collective cheers went up as the group stampeded toward the dining room table. Jade stood there, dumbfounded. By them. By their generosity. By their sheer numbers.

Sawyer snagged her elbow as he passed. There was so much noise, feet and chairs shuffling, laughter and tomfoolery, she didn't catch much of the conversation.

But she let him lead her into the fray, her brain whirling with a paradigm shift.

Was this the way life was meant to be lived? Was this how Christians were supposed to act?

Sawyer jostled her left arm and handed over a big bowl of potato salad, his dimple showing. Quinn teased Brady and Abby about living on love, though Brady's plate was piled high with shrimp and vegetables. Charity made a joke about Dan singeing his eyebrows over the smoker while a smiling Karen called him the hero of the barbecue.

They weren't perfect, as she knew from her

investigation, but they were happy and kind and loved each other.

Regardless of her reserve, she liked them. Every last one, but the man on her left more than all, more than she'd intended.

Maybe families were supposed to be like this, and maybe, just maybe, the Buchanons were not the evil, vengeful creatures her father claimed them to be.

Chapter Eleven

A sunny afternoon by the family swimming pool turned to cooler evening and a touch football game on the lawn. At dark, someone flipped on the porch light for one last game. June bugs buzzed the light, beating their brains out on the side of the house.

Men, women, kids, the whole gang except for Sawyer's pregnant sister, galloped and dodged, laughed and cheated in their usual outrageous manner. Even Bailey, after a very long nap, joined the fun. It was good, Sawyer thought as he watched her, to hear her laugh and play like the teenager she was.

With a pat of her growing belly, Allison opted out of the rough-and-tumble game, volunteering instead to stay inside with Ashton. Even though the baby mostly slept, waking only for a bottle and some fever reducer, Allison declared her need of practice.

Jade genuinely seemed to have a good time. And when she bashed into his side with a fearsome block, Sawyer purposely went sprawling on the thick grass.

Laughing the way he'd always wanted to hear, Jade shot out a hand.

He slapped her palm and wrapped his fingers around hers. "You're tougher than you look."

She tossed blond curls, sassy as she yanked him to his feet. "Told you."

They grinned at each other, out of breath, until one of his ornery brothers shoved him from the back.

"Got a good one there, brother." Brady twitched an eyebrow toward Jade.

Sawyer blew off the statement with a joke, though he suspected his big brother was right. "Not bad for a nosy girl."

Jade elbowed him in the ribs. He *oofed* and moved forward, pretending there was more damage than there was.

Dawson jogged up beside them. "Early start in the morning. I'm heading home. Meet you at the Miller house at seven?"

"Us, too," Brady said. "We're still playing catch-up from being gone so long, and I'm meeting the mayor for breakfast. Zoning issues."

Sawyer readjusted from play to work and mentally checked his schedule, glad Brady handled the business end of things. Give him a slab of wood and a hammer any day over schmoozing the mayor. "Gotta stop at the Building Supply first."

Monday began a new workweek, always a busy day.

The party broke up as the adults gathered kids, toys and wet towels from the backyard and tromped inside.

"I'm grateful we didn't have any break-ins this weekend." Positioning himself next to Jade, Sawyer followed the crowd.

"Perhaps you'll have no more construction site damage. The vandal seems to have focused on you personally."

He made a frustrated noise. "Don't remind me."

"You *are* taking the precautions I suggested, aren't you?"

"Sure." Mostly. He was a man. He was annoyed and angry, not afraid.

Whatever the vandal's motive, Sawyer refused to believe someone wished him physical harm. Still, being the target of anyone's fury nagged at him. Who? Who could be doing this? Was it someone he knew? Someone he liked and thought liked him?

Mom came at Jade with a foil-wrapped packet and a Tupperware container. "Sawyer said you have a fridge and a microwave."

"That's very nice of you. Thanks, and thank you for inviting me this afternoon."

His mom patted Jade's shoulder. "You had a rough start to the day. I'm glad the afternoon turned out better."

"Me, too."

"Don't worry about Bailey and Ashton. We'll take good care of them. Tomorrow, I'll bring her by the motel to pick up her things and check out."

"You're very kind. She appears to be in good hands."

Sawyer frowned. *Appears to be?* That was a strange way to put it. Sawyer had no doubt that his mom and dad would be the underpinnings Bailey needed to get her life back on track. But then, Jade was a private investigator, and her suspicion meter never took a day off.

After a few more minutes of conversation, they said their goodbyes and started the drive to the motel.

Jade was quiet on the ride, focusing her attention out the passenger window. He wondered what she was thinking, what she thought of his family, of him.

"I hope the Buchanon clan wasn't too much for you."

She swiveled to face him. "They're very nice."

"Overwhelming?"

"In a good way."

"Yeah, they're awesome. Loud, annoying, nosy but pretty amazing. I'm a blessed man."

"Yes, you are."

The softly spoken words turned his head. In the soft light of the dashboard, Jade's profile was pensive.

"You worrying about Bailey?" His right hand found hers in the darkness.

"A little." She shifted, her capris whispering on his leather upholstery. "She's a good kid, Sawyer. She needs this boost your family is willing to offer, but I have to ask. What do they get out of it?"

He blinked, frowning at the odd question. "I'm not sure I follow."

"No one is that altruistic without reason. What's their motive?"

"Okaaay." He let go of her hand and made the turn into the motel parking area. "If you need a reason, here you go—Hebrews 13, Matthew 25 and a dozen other scriptures I can't remember. God tells us to share what we have with those in need. To take care of our neighbors."

"That simple?"

He wasn't ready to let her go but she opened the passenger door, lighting the interior.

"That simple." He hopped out, speeding around the truck in time to catch her before she hit the ground. He laughed softly as she stumbled against him. Good timing as far as he was concerned.

He dropped an arm loosely over her shoulders and walked her to the door. This area of town wasn't the best and he fretted to know she came and went alone, but she'd stiffen up all prickly again if he said anything.

Only a few cars passed on the street adjacent to the River Roost, though two of them bounced with loud bass music that set his teeth on edge. Somewhere nearby, probably uptown at the main intersection, an eighteen-wheeler downshifted. A dog barked. The warm summer night pulsed, the area around the motel dark except for the flashing vacancy sign.

When they reached Unit Three, Jade unlocked the door and turned to say good-night. "I enjoyed this afternoon. Thank you."

So stiff and formal. Was she nervous? Afraid that he'd kiss her? Afraid he wouldn't?

He certainly wanted to. "Thanks for hanging out with the wild bunch. You held your own pretty well."

Her bee-stung mouth curved. Sawyer's pulse bumped against his collarbone.

Before he could think of a single reason not to, he leaned slowly down and kissed her. Lightly. Tenderly.

Jade's lips were sweet and soft, the way he'd imagined, and she smelled like barbecue and sunshine.

For the briefest second, she tensed, but every bit as quickly she relaxed and tiptoed up to meet him.

Yeah. This was nice. Better than awesome.

He had that *bing-bong* sensation again, his pulse ratcheting, chest warming. His mind chanted her name.

Reluctantly, figuring he should quit while he was ahead, Sawyer ended the kiss and backed away with a quiet "Good night."

In the shadowy light, Jade's eyes were wide but soft and shining. She looked thunderstruck, the way he felt.

"Good night, Sawyer."

She stepped inside, flipped on the light and closed the door in his face. Sawyer waited until he heard the dead bolt slide before he walked away.

Jade couldn't stop touching her lips. Sawyer, as she'd known he would, kissed like a pro. Like a man who'd kissed dozens of women.

Kissed in a way that made her want to snuggle closer and kiss him again and again.

Heart thudding, she peeled back one slat in the window blinds and watched him walk to his truck, watched the vehicle back up, swing around and drive away, headlights sweeping the motel and disappearing into the night.

He'd kissed her with such tenderness, she'd almost wept. But he hadn't pushed for more. He hadn't taken advantage. He hadn't asked to come inside, expecting more than that one devastating touch of his firm, supple, amazing lips.

He had no idea what that simple act of restraint meant to her.

Dropping the foil-wrapped food and her handbag on the bed, Jade crossed to the wavy, scarred mirror and leaned in, hardly recognizing herself. The tough detective had turned to mush.

She looked soft and vulnerable, the way she didn't want to be. And yet, she couldn't deny the rhythm of happiness pulsing through her bloodstream.

She'd allowed Sawyer to invade her citadel, to smile his way into her heart, to share his incredible family. She felt more for the tall carpenter with the movie star looks than she'd ever intended to allow. Danger was all around, but she'd succumbed to his charm.

Like she had with Cam.

She pressed both hands to her face, reliving the kiss and battling her inward demons. Nothing like Cam.

Nothing like Cam.

Sawyer wasn't all charm and no substance. At least, he didn't appear to be. Cam would never have driven Bailey and her baby to the hospital. Cam wouldn't have stopped at the motel door with only a kiss.

She was falling for Sawyer Buchanon. Falling for a charmer.

Sawyer and his family messed with her head. Were they really such good people, altruistic and caring?

What if they knew who her father was? Would they still invite her to their home and freely offer their friendship?

How would they react if they knew she'd deceived them?

Her conscience pinged.

Like Sawyer, the Buchanon family had been nothing but warm and welcoming. She should have been upfront about her family background from the first day.

But if she'd told them the truth, she could have lost the case…and with it, the opportunity to know Sawyer.

Maybe that would have been a good thing.

With a groan, she put the leftovers in the mini fridge and then flopped onto the bed.

Sawyer was more to her than a pretty face and an intriguing case.

He would hate her if he knew she'd lied. Not in words but in deed.

No, he wouldn't. Not Sawyer.

Mind spinning with a mixture of confusion, longing and all the reasons she shouldn't get involved with Sawyer Buchanon, and all the reasons she already was, Jade relived the day's events, snagging on the conversation in Sawyer's pickup truck.

He'd claimed his family had offered assistance to Bailey because of their faith. He had mentioned two scriptures, neither of which was familiar to her. Not surprising since she had never read the Bible for herself. Never wanted to read about the angry, vengeful God who was eager to punish her for every misstep.

But the Buchanons spoke of God as loving and merciful.

Jade rolled to one side and reached into the top drawer of the bedside table. A Gideon Bible lay inside. She'd seen it every time she'd opened the drawer. Seen the book and ignored it.

Now, she withdrew the brown hardback Bible, racking her memory for the mentioned scriptures.

"Hebrews 13." Finding the index, she flipped to the page and read the entire chapter. She snagged on the first two verses about brotherly love and again at verse sixteen. "Do not forget to do good and to share, for with such sacrifices God is well pleased."

The Buchanons wanted to please God by doing good—a motive with which she could find no fault. Everyone wanted to please God, but she'd grown up thinking to do so required perfection and far greater sacrifices than treating others well.

She'd learned the hard way that she could never be perfect. Nobody could be.

Intrigued, she flipped the pages and read the entire Gospel of John. Some of the scriptures were familiar, but she was shocked at how many were not.

Her interpretation of God shifted. Jesus came to heal hearts, to forgive mistakes and erase wrongs. He displayed mercy and compassion to those who asked.

He came not to condemn but to love and forgive.

Jade's eyes teared up. She blinked away the moisture. She was tired, that was all. She should put away this Bible and go to sleep.

But some force tugged at the place deep inside that had been empty, and she read until she fell asleep with the Gideon Bible on her chest.

Early the next morning she headed to Southview, to the familial home she'd vowed to ignore for as long as possible.

Stubborn to a fault. Begrudging. Unforgiving. That was her.

The drive took less than an hour. Jade used the time to pray, something she hadn't done since Cam had beaten her unconscious and left her bleeding on the bedroom floor of their expensive suburban home.

For such a long time, she'd believed God hadn't heard her sobs and pleas for help. But perhaps she'd been wrong. Cam hadn't killed her. He'd broken her in body and spirit but the event had given her the courage to finally leave him. And she'd survived.

She'd awakened this morning with yesterday's revelations on her mind. She remained confused and uncertain, but if she'd misjudged the Buchanons and God, maybe she'd misjudged her family, too.

Regardless of their differing opinions, she loved her family and missed her mother and their talks. Missed her enough to take this morning away from the Buchanon investigation and drive to the Clifton home in Southview.

Maybe she'd been too hard on her family, even her dad. Perhaps she could mend the rift and take steps toward a more positive, healthy relationship. Like the one the Buchanons shared.

When she arrived at the ordinary wood frame house on Connor Street, only her mother was home. The house looked the same as always, tired and worn, but the interior was spotless, the floors shiny, nothing out of place, the way her father liked things. Mama looked the same. Though she was not allowed to work outside the home, she rose before Daddy every morning to fix her hair and makeup, cook breakfast and to make sure the house was perfect—Daddy's socks and dirty towel picked up, his ashtrays emptied and polished.

Daddy couldn't abide an unkempt woman or a messy house.

Even with finances stretched to the limit, Hugh Clifton demanded perfection in his home and expected Mama to make it happen. According to Daddy, the Bible said that a wife was subject to her husband's authority and her only role in life was to marry, bear children and take care of the house, and she better keep her mouth shut and do it right. Control was his middle name.

As a child, Jade hadn't recognized his need for power, his complete domination over his wife and children. Now she did.

Jade hugged her mother hello and pushed the resentful thoughts aside. She'd come to mend, not to rehash old wounds.

"Jade, honey, I'm so happy to see you. I thought—" Tammy shook her tidy blond head. "Never mind. Let's get some tea and catch up on all you've been doing."

Jade followed her mother into the kitchen and sat at the small round table, watching as Mama bustled around, smiling and happy.

Her conscience throbbed. Could something as simple as a visit bring her mother this much pleasure?

"How have you been, Mama? Really."

"Wonderful as always."

As always. A telling phrase.

"But I don't want to talk about me." Ice rattled from the old-fashioned trays and clinked into glasses. "Tell me about you. About what you've been doing. About your friends. Everything."

Jade accepted the tall glass of amber tea and sipped. "Life is busy. I have a few good friends I go out with sometimes. And I love my work as a private investigator."

"I'm still surprised when you say that. My little girl investigating criminals." Tammy faked a shudder. "Such a dangerous business. I pray for your safety every day."

Jade wanted to scoff but kept her expression straight. She'd been in far more danger married to the man her parents had chosen than she'd ever been in law enforcement.

"I'm perfectly safe, Mama, and if I run into a problem, I'm trained to handle myself."

"But you're pretty and feminine and smart as a whip. Surely you could find a more ladylike occupation."

Jade clenched her back teeth, schooling her words. Mama would never understand. To her, a woman's place was in the home. "I like what I do. I'm happy being an investigator."

And a gorgeous, witty man calls me "Nancy Drew" and is showing me what real faith looks like.

"Then I'm happy for you, no matter what your daddy thinks." They shared a conspiratorial look. "We still have a few secrets, don't we?"

"Yes, we do." Like the time Mama had covered for her so she could attend her junior prom.

Warmed, she reached across the table and squeezed her mother's fingers. Mama had guarded her children against their father's moods and secretly pinched pennies from the grocery budget for the extras every teenager craved, simple little things that Hugh felt were unnecessary.

But even Mama had failed to protect Jade from Cam. He'd been a member of the church, the son of an elder, and the most likely to succeed in their high school.

He'd proven them right in that respect. He now owned a shopping mall, among other things. But he no longer owned her.

Sawyer's smiling face flashed in her mind.

Sawyer. Kind and real, charming and funny, a man who went out of his way for other people.

In a gush of words, she admitted, "Mama, I've met someone."

"Someone?" Tammy looked at her over the glass. "As in a man?"

"Yes."

Her mother leaned back in her chair, the concern on her face evident.

"Aren't you going to ask about him? If he's a good man? If he's a Christian?"

"Is he?"

"Yes. The best kind, I think. Not like Daddy."

"Jade!"

"Because of Sawyer, I prayed today, really prayed, and last night I read the Bible for the first time in my life."

Her mother scoffed. "You've read the Bible since you were a child."

"No, Mama. Daddy gave us verses to memorize." *A foolish child is a grief to his father and bitterness to her who bare him.* "Verses he chose. Verses he used to control us. I never read any of the Bible for myself."

The truth of the statement settled over her mother. Tammy's fingers whitened against the glass of amber tea. In a hesitant murmur, she asked, "Are you...in love with this man?"

A spark went off inside Jade, igniting a thought she'd only begun to consider. *Love.* A big word. A bigger emotion and a giant responsibility.

Like fog over the river, love was slowly creeping in, wrapping gentle fingers around her heart.

"I don't know yet. Maybe. I think he cares for me, and he has the most wonderful family."

Her mother's face softened. "Does he make you happy?"

"It's early, and I'm being cautious this time, but yes, he does. I feel alive again when I'm with him. I feel like I matter, as if I'm important."

Tammy took in a long, deep breath and exhaled, letting the corners of her eyes crinkle. "Then good for you."

"You're not mad at me anymore about leaving Cam?"

"I never was mad, honey, only confused and sad, but after we spoke a few days ago, I realized six years is long enough. You have every right to move on with your life and if that includes this man, then I'm glad for you."

"No matter what Daddy thinks?"

"He'd be upset if he knew, but we'll keep this between us for now. Your father doesn't need to know."

"No, he doesn't." At least, not yet.

They exchanged the secret smile again that warmed Jade all the way through. She was glad she'd come. Glad to see Mama. "Is he at work?"

Tammy cast a nervous glance toward the door. "He went to town for a while."

"What happened to the job at the nursing home?"

"You know your daddy. Maintenance work is below him. Hugh owned his own company. He'll never be satisfied with menial employment."

Jade's mouth tightened but she didn't say the obvious. Any work was better than nothing. "So he's unemployed again?"

"Temporarily." Tammy emitted a tired sigh. "He'll find something to tide us over until he gets his company going again. He always does."

Tide them over. For as long as Jade could remember, they barely got by—the fault of every Buchanon on the planet, of course.

Jade longed to ask about the lawsuit Dan Buchanon filed against Clifton Construction some years ago. As confident as she was that Sawyer's "special girl" was also their vandal, a pinch of doubt lingered. If her own flesh and blood was involved in the vandalism, seeking revenge for perceived wrongs done to Hugh Clifton and his company, she needed to know. Discovering the truth was her job.

She had to find out before Sawyer learned she was Hugh Clifton's daughter. Maybe he would understand but what if he didn't? What if he despised her deceit? He was, he'd told her on more than one occasion, an upfront kind of man. No secrets.

And she had too many.

Readjusting the napkin beneath her tea glass, Jade determined to get the truth and share that truth with Sawyer. Somehow.

"Was Daddy always…" She wanted to say *angry, vengeful, volatile,* but those words would upset her mother, so she rephrased. "What was Daddy like when you first met?"

Mama's expression brightened. "He was the handsomest man I'd ever seen. Sweet and funny."

"Daddy? Funny?"

"Oh, yes, he had a great sense of humor. All the

girls were after him, and I was so flattered when he picked me. I fell hard."

Jade propped her chin on her fist and leaned in, intrigued by this revelation. "Tell me about your courtship. How did he treat you?"

She wanted to ask if he was controlling and abusive even then. She needed to know if all men began with smiles and ended with slaps.

"He sent me flowers and candy and was forever telling me how pretty I was." Mama touched her sleek French knot. "He loved my long blond hair and said I should never cut anything so beautiful."

"And you never have."

"Why would I when long hair makes my husband happy?" Mama sipped her tea, nostalgic. "I'd never met such an attentive, charming man, and when he proposed, I jumped at the chance to be his wife."

Charming. A word that scared Jade.

"Was he ever…rough with you when you were dating?"

"No. Not once." Mama picked at the napkin beneath her glass.

"What happened?" She didn't have to elaborate. Her mother understood what she was asking: *When had the slaps and shoves begun?*

Tammy grew pensive, staring across the kitchen at the ancient refrigerator they'd had since Jade was a child. "Life hasn't been easy for your father. When he lost his company—"

"Even before then, he didn't treat you right." Although Hugh hadn't hit her in the early days, Tammy Clifton had been ridiculed and put down and made to appear stupid and inadequate for as long as Jade could remember.

His cruel words and the tension in their home had been the reason Jade jumped into marriage with Cam. She'd thought Cameron Warren was all the things her father wasn't. Now she knew her father had been kind and loving in the beginning, too.

Was Sawyer the same? Was he another case of Jekyll and Hyde?

She didn't want to believe it, but she was too smart not to be cautious.

"Things happen in a marriage, I guess," Mama was saying. "Disappointments. Misunderstandings. Inadequacies. I considered his jealousy a compliment. He didn't want to share me."

"But he was wonderful when you dated?"

"Yes, he was, and someday, when he gets his company going again, he'll be the man I fell in love with."

Would he be? Or was there something elemental broken inside her father?

"What's going on in here?"

The male voice stunned them both. They

turned toward the barrel-chested man entering the kitchen.

How much of their conversation had he overheard?

Mama hopped to her feet, flustered, guilty. "Hugh, look who's here. Our Jade drove all the way from Paris to see us."

Jade didn't bother to correct her mother's mistake. She'd driven from Gabriel's Crossing, not Paris.

"Hi, Daddy." Out of habit, she stood to her feet. Daddy commanded respect from his children.

He swept a glance across her but spoke to his wife. "Get me some tea. It's hot out there."

At his curt tone of voice, Jade thought of the way Dan Buchanon treated his wife, of his affectionate tone, his appreciation for the things she did. Brady and Jake treated their wives well, too.

She had been, she knew, soured on men as husbands, though rationally she understood that not all husbands were harsh masters over their servant wives. Not like her father.

Even now, Tammy hurried to do her husband's bidding, taking ice trays from the freezer in a rush. As she held them over the sink and broke out the cubes, she looked over one shoulder. "How was your meeting?"

Jade watched her father's face. She knew the signs, felt the crackle of tension. He was in a bad mood. No big surprise there.

"A bust." He sat down across from Jade. She slid back onto her chair, disappointed that there would be no lovely family reunion. She shouldn't have expected one.

Tammy bustled to Hugh's side with the filled glass.

He pushed it away. "You know I like plenty of ice."

Temper prickled the hair on Jade's neck. For her mother's sake, she kept her lips clamped tightly.

The fridge opened and closed and ice plopped. "Sorry, honey. I was so excited to see Jade, I wasn't thinking. Is this better? Would you like something to eat with it? I made oatmeal cookies, your favorite."

Without responding, Hugh took the glass and drank deeply. "Stupid bank won't float the equipment loan."

"Why not?"

"Bad economy, financial risk. Even though I explained the bankruptcy again for the hundredth time, they didn't budge." He slammed the glass against the tabletop. "Sorry Buchanons. This is their fault."

Her mother jumped. She hovered around the table, on her feet, wringing a dish towel in her hands.

Anger bubbled in Jade's chest. She tamped it down, kept her tone conversational. This was her opportunity and she wouldn't ruin it with a fight.

"Why, Daddy? Why is this the Buchanons' fault? Wasn't that a long time ago?"

Steel-gray eyes slanted toward her, hard and cold. "Do you see any concrete trucks in the driveway? No, you don't. Thanks to them, I sold everything the bank didn't take."

"I know, Daddy. I know, but help me understand what happened."

"Why bother? They're like a cancer. Once they invade, they suck the life out of a man."

"But that was years ago. Why does it matter now?"

Her mother paused behind her chair to squeeze her shoulder in a silent plea to stop talking.

She couldn't. While keeping her knowledge to herself, she pushed the topic, needing to know, needing to settle in her heart the issue of which was the guilty party.

"What did the Buchanons do that was so terrible?"

"Ran me out of business. Bad-mouthed my hard work, told other builders not to use my company. You know all that."

"Maybe they thought they had good reason."

Her mother's fingers tightened on her shoulders, tightened and held.

Hugh's eyes narrowed to slits. "What are you talking about, girly? What good reason could they have for ruining a man except they're plain evil?"

"The lawsuit."

Her father's face reddened to purple. His eyes bulged. "Don't you come into my house disrespecting me."

Honor thy father and mother ran through Jade's head like a knife blade. Any moment now, Hugh would blast her with all the scriptural reasons why she was wrong and he was right. A child should never have an opinion, especially a female child.

Jade softened her tone but didn't retreat. She'd faced scarier men during her cop days.

"I don't mean disrespect, Daddy. I'm only trying to understand."

"Then understand this. Dan Buchanon is a worthless piece of trash who stole everything we ever had!" His voice rising with his body, he leaned across the table to jab a thick finger in Jade's face. "Don't you ever let me hear you defend him again. Now shut your mouth or get out!"

Icy cold and heavyhearted, Jade rose from the table, set her half-emptied glass in the sink and hugged her mother goodbye.

So much for thinking she could mend fences.

Chapter Twelve

You kissed that blonde witch. I saw you. She came on to you, pushing up against you, trying to lure you inside the motel. She disgusts me. Stop seeing her. My love is strong, but I cried myself to sleep last night. Does that make you sad? Like the paint on your truck? Did you cry? Are you sorry? Sorry you cheated? I forgive you, my darling. Forgiveness is the price of love. Don't do it again. You'll have to pay.

Sawyer gazed in fascinated horror at the rambling pink letter found under his truck's wiper blade.

Who was this person? And how did she know he'd kissed Jade outside the River Roost last night?

His fingers tightened on the sheet.

"She admits spray painting my truck! This, this—" He was sputtering as he found the signature on the back page halfway down. The same person who wrote the rambling emails. "Special Girl."

The idea that someone might be watching his every move had him turning in a slow circle, suddenly paranoid. The only other people he saw on his quiet residential street were two men on the golf course and the older widow, Mrs. French, three houses down watering her flowers.

His neighborhood remained peaceful. No signs of a mad stalker, though now that he knew she'd been to his home, peeked in windows, left a note on his windshield and watched him kiss Jade, he could get seriously freaked out.

Anyone who wrote secret, bizarre notes and vandalized property out of "love" couldn't be emotionally stable. Was she insane? Dangerous? Outright evil? Or simply mean and vindictive?

He jabbed the office number into his phone.

"Speak." Quinn was never one for long hellos.

"Is everyone okay over there?"

"Sure. Why wouldn't we be?"

Sawyer turned another slow circle in his driveway, aware that his adrenaline had jacked and hair rose on the back of his neck. "I found a note on my truck."

"More graffiti?"

"No, an actual handwritten note under the wiper blade. Rambling, creepy. She knew I was with Jade last night and wasn't at all happy. She made some veiled threats."

A beat passed. "Are you in danger?"

"Probably not." He gave a short laugh. "She says she loves me. Me and my pretty face."

"So she paints your truck and leaves threatening notes. Some love."

"Tell me about it."

"You have no idea who this woman is?"

"None. Jade says she uses a false profile on social media."

"Eerie. Unsettling. You think your admirer and the vandal are connected?"

How could they be? This woman claimed to love him. Love didn't destroy. And yet she'd painted his truck with obscenities.

"I'm not sure. Maybe. Maybe not. Jade thinks it's possible, even though I haven't heard directly from this woman until now and the vandalism has been going on for a couple of years."

"Either way, better call Leroy."

"Yeah. Yeah." Sawyer shoved a hand over his hair. "I'd rather Mom didn't know about this. She'll worry about me."

"Got it. And, brother—"

"Yeah?"

"Watch your back."

A chill prickled Sawyer's spine as he hung up. He gave the police chief a quick call and then dialed Jade. That he wanted to see her anyway was a bonus, but right now the focus was this nutty, rambling, semicoherent letter that went on for two miserable pages.

Jade answered on the third ring. "Hello."

"Hey. It's me, Sawyer."

"I know." She didn't sound too friendly.

"You okay? Is everything all right?"

"Why wouldn't I be?" Her speech was terse, snappy.

Okaaay. Was she angry about last night's kiss? Regretting it? Wishing he'd go away?

Sawyer titled his head back and stared at the fluffy white clouds. He spotted Moses with a staff, like he might have during a game he and his twin had played as boys. Find the picture in the clouds.

He wished he could as easily find a balance with Jade.

"Can you come over to my house? I need to show you something."

"I'm busy. Is this related to the case?"

Whoa. Sherlock was back, cool and professional.

"Yes, but what happened to the woman I was with last night?"

"Excuse me?"

He squinched his eyes shut. "Did I do something to upset you?"

"Of course not. I'm out of town visiting family. This is a bad time."

That explained her brusque tone. She didn't mean anything by it. She was preoccupied.

"I found a bizarre note on my windshield."

"From Special Girl?"

"How did you guess?"

She didn't humor him with a response. "Call the police."

"I did."

There was a pause on the other end of the line.

He heard a noise in the background that sounded like traffic.

Did her family live in the middle of a busy highway?

"I'll be back into town tonight, around seven. I'll come by your place then, have a look at the note and discuss business."

"Can we discuss happy things, too?"

Silence.

"Jade."

"Yes."

"I want to see you again. You. Not Nancy Drew."

She hung up without responding.

Sawyer stared at the cell phone for fifteen seconds, puzzled by her cool, curt behavior. After her dogged attempts to solve this case, Sawyer thought she'd be thrilled to have a new clue.

Not that *he* was all that happy about the latest installment. Having a demented secret admirer gave a man serious pause.

But ever the optimist, Sawyer looked on the

bright side. Jade was coming over tonight. He didn't understand why she'd suddenly become distant when he thought things were really taking off between them, but maybe she had other things on her mind. A person got distracted around family. He certainly did.

"Admit it, man." With the pink note in hand, he sat down on his front porch to await Leroy. "You're falling for her."

With a laugh, he nodded, aware that if his stalker was watching him talk to himself, she'd think he was as nutty as her.

He wished Jade was here now. Last night, he'd fallen asleep with her taste on his lips and their wonderful afternoon on his mind. His dreams had been sweet and filled with her.

He was falling for a woman who only liked him on alternate Sundays. Or less.

Nah, that wasn't true. She was only trying to maintain her professional distance. When she interacted with his family and with him on a personal level, she was warm and fun. Real warm.

He revisited last night's kiss and her reaction. He wasn't naive. She'd felt something, too. Something *bing-bong* big.

Love. He'd been in *like* a hundred times, but love had evaded him.

Beautiful Jade had him by the heart and he didn't mind one bit.

Now, if only she would cooperate.

* * *

Jade's back ached with tension as she guided her Chevy across the Red River Bridge. The swirling muddy water below mirrored her thoughts and emotions.

Her father would never change. Why did she think a few prayers and her new attitude toward God and family would make any difference?

But she wanted it to make a difference so badly. She wanted a family like Sawyer's. She wanted to believe God cared about her.

The radio played country music but she barely noticed.

Sawyer had called. Something about a note from his secret admirer.

Simply hearing his voice had cheered her. She wanted to believe Sawyer was nothing like Cam or her father.

After today, how could she ever be sure?

From Mama's description, Daddy was sweet and charming before the marriage…the way Cam had been. Charmers, both of them, like Sawyer.

Men presented one personality when they wanted a woman. Once they had her, they turned to monsters.

Like multicolored beads on a string, a few cars and trucks motored past. When a faded blue Dodge Ram came into sight, her stomach tightened.

Her brother Bo drove a truck like that. She

squinted as the truck sailed past, recognizing Bo in the driver's seat and Kurt next to him.

What were her brothers doing near Gabriel's Crossing?

She punched off the radio, needing to clear her mind of thoughts of Sawyer so she could really think. This bridge connected Oklahoma and Texas. Bo and Kurt could be heading home from anywhere. Their presence could be perfectly innocent. Or they could have been in Gabriel's Crossing for a more sinister reason—to avenge their father, to punish the Buchanons, to destroy another Buchanon Built property.

Gripping the steering wheel in a choke hold, she accelerated toward Sawyer's house.

He met her at the door, all smiles and sweetness. Clean shaven and smelling really good, he wore slacks and a button-down shirt as if he'd planned an evening out.

"You made it."

Nerves about to snap and trying not to ask where he was headed, she blurted, "Was there another break-in today?"

Expression puzzled, he shook his head. "No. Why?"

"Are you sure?"

"Positive."

She gave a curt nod. Get the note, get out and let him be on his way. That was a better scenario anyway. The more she was with him the more she wanted to be.

"Show me this note you received."

"Hey, slow down, Nancy." He took her hand and tugged her through the door. "I've waited all day to see you again. The note can wait."

Inside the house was quiet, dim and cool, a welcome respite from Texas heat.

She was here on business. She was an investigator. He didn't know the truth about her family.

"But you're going somewhere." She struggled for cool professionalism but Sawyer's touch distracted her, warmed her, made her yearn to be with him on a personal level.

He chuckled softly. "No, I'm not. Come here. I want to show you something."

There was nothing she could do but follow as he led her through the tidy living room into the dim kitchen-dining area. Jade stopped in the doorway, stunned.

She noticed then what she'd been too preoccupied to observe when he'd first opened the door. The house smelled as good as Sawyer, only the scents were food.

And the dining room had been transformed into a cozy, romantic setting for two.

A chunky candle glowed white atop a small linen-covered table set with cherry-red placemats and silverware. Across one gleaming white plate, he'd placed a long-stemmed red rose. Soft instrumental music floated from somewhere.

Jade's heart bumped against her rib cage. "Sawyer, what are you doing? What's going on?"

"Surprise." His voice was soft and gentle.

"This is for me?" He wasn't going out. Nor was he expecting some gorgeous redhead for dinner. He'd done this for her.

If she hadn't been a wreck before, she was now.

"For us. You sounded upset on the phone. Stressed. Uptight. I thought a nice, relaxing dinner…" His words dwindled, his expression a mix of pride and uncertainty.

The uncertainty endeared him to her even more.

"It's beautiful." And romantic. Way too romantic. She loved it.

Oh, dear.

"I should really see that note." Her tone wasn't the least bit cool and professional.

"Gave it to Leroy. We'll look at a copy later. Right now you need to relax." His strong carpenter's fingers found her shoulders and massaged. "Tight as Dick's hatband." His laugh was soft against her ear, sending shivers. "I have no idea what that means but Dad says it."

She gave herself to his talented fingers and let her head loll forward. She shouldn't, but he was right—today's confrontation with her father and the disappointment that followed had tied her into a thousand hard knots.

"You went to visit your family today. Did something happen to upset you?"

His radar was right on.

"Something always happens with them. My dad—" She bit down on her lip and shook her head, stepping away from his delicious touch, reluctant to share her problems with a man who came from the perfect environment. "You wouldn't understand."

But he was having none of it. "Try me. I'm a pretty good listener and a great shoulder if you need one."

Leaning on Sawyer's broad shoulders sounded wonderful. She couldn't allow herself to be that weak and needy.

Two are better than one. Wasn't that what he'd told her? Because if one fell down, the other was there to give a hand up.

Was that the way marriage was for his parents? Partners. Helping each other? Or was such a relationship nothing but a romantic fantasy?

"Come and sit." He pulled the chair away from the table. "I'll fix your drink and you can tell me all about it. Then we'll let the stress burn up in that candle flame while we enjoy the dinner I slaved over for hours." He flashed his teasing, breathtaking smile. "Deal?"

When he put it like that, how could she refuse?

After seating her, he moved around his kitchen with ease. He glanced in the oven and gave a pleased hum before bringing two tall drinks to the table. A sprig of mint garnished each glass.

"I hope you like blackberry tea."

She'd never had it but she took a sip. "Light, refreshing. Perfect." Like him. Too perfect.

He slid two salad plates onto the table and joined her, his handsome face shadowy and romantic in the candlelight as he leaned toward her. "Want to tell me what got you so upset?"

She sighed and sat back, hands in her lap. "My father and I had words. We always do. That's all. Not worth discussing."

"I'm sorry." He smoothed out his napkin and jabbed a fork into the green salad. "Fathers can be exacting sometimes."

"Not yours." She picked up her fork and began to eat.

"Oh, yes, he can. He and Brady butt heads on a regular basis, and I've had my moments with him."

"But you get along so well together."

"Well, sure we do. We're family. We disagree and then we kiss and make up and have a cookout." The corner of his mouth lifted. "Maybe not the kissing part so much anymore, but we fix the problem and move forward."

"My family doesn't do that. They hold grudges forever. With each other. With everyone else. Especially with those who've done them wrong."

The truth hovered on her tongue, a winged creature demanding to fly.

"Want to talk about your argument? What started things off on the wrong foot?"

"I don't want to talk about it all." She lifted a bite of mixed salad. "This dressing is delicious. Did you make it?"

"No, but I made the money that bought it."

She laughed outright, feeling the day's stress slowly seep from her shoulders. Sawyer had that effect on her, as if being with him made everything all right.

"Whatever you have in the oven smells incredible. Did you make the money that bought that, too?"

"I did. But I also baked it, with a little help from my baby sister." He rubbed his palms together and intoned like the best maître d'. "Slow-baked salmon with lemon and thyme, served alongside parmesan asparagus."

"Sounds fancy."

"Are you suitably impressed?"

"I haven't tasted it yet."

He laughed. "Spoken like a Buchanon."

While she absorbed that tempting phrase, the oven beeped and he hopped up to plate and serve the meal, taking time to refill her glass before he rejoined her.

She had never seen her father fill her mother's

glass. Certainly, Daddy had never cooked a meal or prepared Mama's plate. Not in her lifetime.

With the candle flickering between them, they talked as they ate. To her relief they moved from the subject of her family to Bailey and Ashton who were now settled in Karen and Dan's extra apartment.

"I'll miss having the pair of them right down the walkway from me."

"Which means you'll have to come to more Sunday dinners so you can see them."

"I'd like that."

"Church, too?"

"Maybe." Jade sipped her tea. "Your interpretation of God is different from the way I was raised. But I like yours better and I've been reading the Gideon Bible in my motel room, trying to decide…which is the real God?"

"Good question. Mine is, of course." The grin flashed but he was serious. "Keep reading that Bible, Jade. Read the first four books of the New Testament. Watch Jesus at work, the way He treated people, the love and compassion He displayed."

"But that was Jesus."

"Christ said, 'If you've seen me, you've seen the Father.'"

"The Bible says that?"

"Yep. Don't get me wrong. God is a god of justice and can't tolerate sin. He doesn't have an attitude of 'anything goes,' but above all else He loves. In fact, He's the embodiment of love." Sawyer lifted one shoulder in a mini shrug. "Sorry, if I'm coming on too strong. I'm pretty passionate about Jesus."

She waved her fork, showing him that he hadn't. "You've given me a lot to think about. And pray about. I appreciate your input. But can we get back to Bailey and Ashton?"

Talking about religion was something she'd avoided for a long time. Sawyer and his family had opened her eyes to an appealing Christianity but she needed time to process and study for herself. Never again would she take anyone's word for what the Bible said.

"Absolutely."

His lips curved, blue eyes aglow in the candlelight. Sawyer was devastatingly handsome, and once she'd worked her way beyond the happy-go-lucky facade, she discovered a man of intellect and deep character. Who would have guessed there was so much behind that movie star face?

"I stopped by Mom's this afternoon to check on them. Ashton is a heart grabber." He thumped a fist against his chest. "Gets me right there."

"You like kids." She'd seen the way he played with his nieces and nephews, the way he listened to their chatter and made them feel important. He'd even toted each in turn on a piggyback gallop around the backyard and tossed them around in the swimming pool.

Sawyer Buchanon would make a terrific father.

"Adore them. Want a few of them myself some-day. Maybe not as many as Mom and Dad had..." His gaze held hers over the flickering candle. "How about you?"

So much for sidestepping difficult topics. From religion to babies—a tough transition. A cloak of the past shrouded her for a brief moment while she sought balance. She lowered her eyes to the salmon, surprised at how much she'd eaten.

Sawyer couldn't know how the question of chil-dren stirred painful memories.

"Hey." He reached across the table and tilted her chin upward. "Did I say something wrong? You don't like kids?"

"I love kids." Her lip trembled. She bit it but not before Sawyer noticed.

His brow puckered. "Why do you look so sad? What's wrong?"

She didn't talk about the loss. Never had, not even to her closest friends.

Two are better than one. Bear one another's burdens.

Suddenly, the need to share her heartache was overwhelming and the dim lighting provided a cover that fostered intimacy. She could tell him. Sawyer was a good listener.

Jade sat back in the chair with a heavy sigh, a deep ache in her soul throbbing for release.

Keeping her voice cool and professional, while her heart rattled against her rib cage, she said the forbidden words. "I had a miscarriage a few years ago, courtesy of my ex."

Sawyer's scowl deepened. "What do you mean, *courtesy* of your ex?"

Her pulse pounded so hard, she thought her collarbone might snap. "He didn't want children. He was furious when I told him. We had a huge fight. He won."

She tried to sound matter-of-fact, but her lips trembled again and tears burned the back of her nose.

Slowly, slowly, Sawyer put aside his fork and rose to his feet, coming around the table to kneel next to her chair. He took her hand, warming it between both of his.

"Are you saying what I think you are?"

She licked dry, dry lips. Candle flame flickered as if her inner turmoil stirred the air. "He beat me unconscious. When I came to, I called 911. Cam was gone. An ambulance took me to the hospital. I lost the baby."

At the time, she'd blamed herself. She'd known he didn't want children. She'd foolishly thought he'd change his mind when he learned she was pregnant. Now, she knew better. Cam was selfish, angry and broken, and nothing she did would fix him.

Sawyer growled low and deep, a primal sound, before tugging her into his arms where he rocked her back and forth like a child. A wall of fear and caution began to crumble as she rested in his accepting embrace.

Compassion poured from him. He murmured comfort and words tender enough to melt the coldest iceberg.

This man melted her, made her feel safe and valued.

The tears came then. Tears she'd held back since the kind-faced physician in Southview had confirmed her suspicions of miscarriage.

"Cry, my love. It's okay. I've got you."

He let her cry while he smoothed his hand over her hair, down her back, murmuring, making promises not to let anyone ever hurt her again. She wished he could keep that promise, that she dared trust him.

She'd learned the hard way not to depend on a man. A woman had to protect herself. But in this moment, the words soothed a raw, aching wound, and she let them pour over her like warm rain.

When the torrent passed, she shuddered a few times and tried to pull away, embarrassed, though strangely relieved, as if the tears had washed out toxins she hadn't known were there. "I'm sorry. I never do that."

Had she ever let herself cry for her lost baby?

"Don't apologize. I'm here for you." Sawyer cupped her face and kissed away the remaining tears before finding her lips with his.

The kiss was gentle and compassionate, but leashed passion hovered in the wings. His heart ricocheted against hers, his restraint meaning more to her than he'd ever know. She'd never met a man with self-control, one that thought of her first and himself second.

Sawyer was a different kind of man, and the truth of that both thrilled and terrified her. Would he always be this way, or would he change?

He eased back a little, held her face close to his and whispered, "I'm falling in love with you, Jade." His breath brushed her lips in a soft, self-deprecating laugh. "I guess that's obvious."

The rattle in her chest shot into her brain. Her blood pressure jacked. Adrenaline flooded through her body. Fight or flight.

With every fiber of her being, Jade wanted to believe he was the man he presented to her to-night. She wanted to believe he wouldn't change with the first disagreement.

But would he turn into a monster when he discovered who she really was? That her family might be the cause of his family's problems?

As much as she wanted to let go and feel all the beautiful emotions banking up inside like a brewing summer rain, she couldn't take the chance.

Requiring every ounce of willpower she had, Jade levered away from Sawyer's tempting arms, thanked him politely for the nice dinner and, over his bewildered protests, escaped into the hot, muggy Texas night.

Chapter Thirteen

Jade slept little that night. She sprawled on the bed listening to the humming pipes in the next unit and loud music thump from the adjacent street while wondering what she'd gotten herself into.

Sawyer loved her? Really?

Reliving those moments in his arms was torture and pure delight.

With a groan, she flipped on the light, took her computer from beneath the mattress and opened the Buchanon file.

Then, and only then, she remembered the reason for her visit to Sawyer's house. Not to tell him her sad story. Not to be wined and dined with a romantic dinner. Not even to hear him say those beautiful words that replayed in her head like a melody.

The note from Sawyer's stalker. In her haste and confusion, she'd forgotten all about the note.

Frustrated, she slapped a hand against her forehead. The note could be information vital to solving this case and relieve her fear that her family was involved in the break-ins. The note could lead to the stalker, the vandal.

She was losing her perspective, her professionalism. Sawyer and a volley of rampant emotions compromised her ability to do her job.

She needed to finish this investigation, find the culprit and get away while she still had a brain cell left in her head.

Next to her brother's name, she typed, Spotted Bo near Gabriel's Crossing. Could he have written the note and left it on Sawyer's truck to draw attention away from himself, the true vandal? She had no proof that the stalker was real or even that the person who wrote the note was a woman. Bo could have done the damage to Sawyer's truck as well as vandalizing the Buchanon properties. He could be using the stalker concept to throw investigators off the scent. Was her brother clever enough to concoct such a scheme?

Stomach sinking, she admitted the awful truth. Between the three of them, her brothers and her father could easily be to blame. And her job was to find out and report them to the police.

The next morning, Jade rose after less than three hours of restless sleep, gritty-eyed but determined. She texted Sawyer and asked him to meet her with the note. Sawyer probably thought she was nuts, the way she'd run out on him last night.

Sawyer's reply named The Buttered Biscuit Café in fifteen minutes. Good. A neutral location in public. No way would she return to his town house and the rush of romantic emotions, but she must complete this investigation. She *had* to learn if her family was involved.

Taking her time in the shower, Jade procrastinated, putting off the inevitable moment when she'd have to face Sawyer again.

She'd been anything but professional last night. Today, she would be. Cool. Confident. Professional.

By the time she finally walked inside the café, she was late and the room was thick with people and delicious smells, bacon and Jan's cat-head biscuits. Jade's mouth pooled with hunger as she found Sawyer among the crowd.

He waited at a square table next to a window, iced orange juice in front of him. The blinds at his elbow were closed against the morning sun and he spotted her immediately. He didn't smile.

Guilt clenched at her as their gazes met and held. He looked puzzled…and hurt. She'd done that. She'd stolen the laughter from a happy man.

She yearned to tell him everything, to spill out the truth the way she'd told him of the miscarriage, to make him smile again. To admit she was falling in love with him, too.

Don't take the chance. Don't be vulnerable. Don't be a fool.

Excusing her way past the filled tables, she approached him. He stood, gentlemanlike, which only compounded her guilt.

"You okay?" he asked, softly.

His look of concern almost did her in. Why did he have to do that? Why did he have to appear concerned for her well-being after she had performed her Houdini act and disappeared?

A little voice in her head whispered, "Because he's the real deal."

She glanced down, away from those piercing eyes. "I'm fine."

"Are you sure? You look tired." He pulled out a chair and gestured. "Sit. I ordered your breakfast."

There he went again. Considerate and thoughtful. Or was he being controlling and pushy?

The thought scared her. "No need. I only came for the note."

The waitress appeared with coffee and poured without asking. "Pancakes and bacon will be up in a minute. Want anything else with that? The blackberry syrup is on the table."

Dumbly, she shook her head. He'd ordered foods she loved. She was hungry. She might as well eat.

The strain at the table nearly palpable, she searched for something to say. "Pancakes with blackberry syrup are my favorite."

"I know. Bacon, too."

He'd remembered their passing conversation about favorite foods? He was an omelet man, Southwestern style with plenty of jalapeños and onions and an unbelievably huge glob of hot salsa.

Charla flashed by and deposited two steaming plates on the table. "You all need anything else?"

Sawyer lifted an eyebrow toward Jade. She shook her head.

"We're good for now, Charla. Thank you."

Charla gave his biceps a playful tweak. "Don't forget to leave me a big tip. You know I'm worth it."

He laughed, and Jade was grateful for the feisty waitress.

After Charla bustled away, last night pulsed between them, unspoken. While they ate, they talked of mundane things, impersonal, distant, the way she wanted them to be. Though her thoughts were on last night and how bewildered he must be, Jade focused on the note and the investigation, digging deeper into even the most innocent friendships he shared with women.

She prayed there was something in his past relationships, anything that would stir a personal vendetta.

It had to be that. It simply had to be. The alternative was too upsetting.

All the while, her blood thrummed with the

fear that her brother, not an unrequited lover, had written the note and spray painted Sawyer's truck.

Installing crown molding above a set of custom-built birch cabinets in the Carter house should have kept Sawyer's mind off Jade Warren. It didn't.

Finish nails in hand, Sawyer mulled Jade's bizarre behavior from last night and this morning's return to the cool, impersonal detective. A detective who had kissed him like she meant it.

What had happened?

One minute, he'd said the three gargantuan words he'd never said to anyone and the next she'd bolted like a startled rabbit. He'd thought they were beyond that.

Nail between index finger and thumb, he slammed the hammer down...onto his hand.

With a yelp, he dropped the tools and shook his clenched hand. He hadn't hammered himself in years.

"What's going on with you today?" Dawson, working from the other wall, paused midhammer.

Sawyer glared at the insulted skin, already beginning to bruise. "Nothing. Why?"

"You're too quiet. Makes me suspicious. Now you're banging your hand like an amateur."

"Got a lot on my mind." He retrieved the finish hammer and slipped it through the loop on his tool belt.

Nails rattled as Dawson withdrew a handful from the box on the counter. "The stalker?"

"Partly."

"Ah." His intuitive twin pinned him with a look, nodding sagely. "Jade. Want to talk about her?"

Sawyer scowled. "No."

Jade had effectively given him the cold shoulder. He wasn't one who liked to discuss being rejected, especially when he didn't know why. Not even with his twin.

Unless his girl-guy radar was seriously out of whack, Jade liked him. A lot. Or she had. Last night she'd been enjoying herself, once she'd relaxed from whatever had happened with her father. Then she'd shared a deep, painful event with him, one that had him wanting to comfort her and take a hammer to her ex. She liked him. She trusted him with her pain. Something special was growing between them.

And yet all she'd wanted to talk about this morning was the case, his former girlfriends, his unknown stalker.

He was tired of the whole mess, tired of looking over his shoulder, of wondering if every friend he spoke to was sabotaging him behind his back. Most of all, he was tired of Jade's hot and cold behavior. She was enough to give him a head cold.

He didn't like living this way.

"I can finish this up if you want to knock off for

the day." Dawson flipped over a length of molding and positioned it along the wall.

Sawyer ran a hand over the back of his neck and winced. The thumb throbbed like a gangsters' set of Bose subwoofers. "Thanks. I think I will. I'm worthless anyway."

"I'll lock up, but don't leave your saw."

They'd had too many things stolen, even a landscaper's skid-steer, which was later recovered in the woods. How the vandal had started and moved the large piece of equipment without being seen baffled them all.

Sawyer removed his tool bag and tossed the overloaded leather onto the counter with a loud *thunk*. "Bathroom cabinets tomorrow?"

"If you're up to it." Dawson's grin teased. "Go see Jade. Let her kiss that thumb and make it all better."

"Stuff it, Dawson." Though the idea didn't sound half-bad.

Outside he slapped the sawdust from his clothes and loaded his saw and other major tools before hopping into his truck.

The thumb throbbed. His head hurt, and yes, his heart hurt.

In town, he stopped at the IGA for milk and contemplated a fast-food dinner. He could always go over to Mom's for a home-cooked meal.

Nah, Mom would know something was wrong. Her mother radar never took a day off. And he wasn't up to cooking again. A sandwich would have to do.

He really wanted to see Jade.

Was he ever messed up!

He flipped on K-LOVE Radio, hoping the positive music would encourage him, and as he drove, he prayed. God knew what was going on even if Sawyer was in the dark.

The big diesel pickup rumbled into the garage and he cut the engine and walked out to the mailbox on the curb.

His *Master Builder* magazine lay curled inside along with a couple of bills. "And enough junk mail to destroy the Brazilian rain forest."

As he walked toward the front door, he scanned the new magazine and distractedly jiggled his key into the lock.

Inside, he tossed the mail onto a side table, flipped on the light...and froze.

His living room looked like a monument to ransacking. Tours on the hour.

End tables turned over, lamps smashed, pictures torn from the walls and frames broken. His television was muted, news of a bombing flickering, and red paint scrawled across the walls and his fifty-two-inch TV screen.

I warned you.

Guts knotted, neck tense, he listened for a hint that the perpetrator was still inside his home.

Nothing. All he heard was his own heartbeat, loud, rapid.

His adrenaline leaping like a Jack Russell terrier, Sawyer backed out of the house and went to his truck, dialing 911 as he went. Hammer in hand, he returned and explored both floors.

Whoever had done this was gone.

He stalled out at the bottom of the stairs, sucked oxygen and considered if he was relieved to be alone or furious to have not found the culprit.

Jaw tight, he pressed ten on his cell phone, Jade's speed dial number.

Yeah, he'd put her on speed dial.

After too many rings that told him she wasn't excited to talk to him, she answered. "Hello."

"You'd better get over to my place right away."

She must have heard the urgency in his voice because she didn't argue. "What happened?"

"The stalker paid me a visit. It isn't pretty."

A sharp intake of breath. "Get out of the house."

"No need. It's clear."

"You shouldn't have checked."

"Too bad. I did." He was a man and he wanted to know who was doing this to him. "I have a hammer."

She snorted. "Call the police."

"I already have."

"On my way."

She arrived in less than five minutes and burst through the front door without knocking.

He whirled at the sound, hammer aloft and then, annoyed to be jumpy, lowered the weapon. He'd never before considered his tools as weapons, but yeah, they came in handy.

"Are you all right?" Nancy Drew was all business. He didn't like it.

"I am. My house isn't."

Her eyes roved over the topsy-turvy clutter, settling on the television. He saw her mind work through the details.

"Is she saying the note from yesterday was a warning?"

"What do you think?" The first disturbing paragraph was indelibly imprinted in his brain. He'd been warned in no uncertain terms to stay away from Jade.

"She warned you about—" Jade's cheeks reddened "—me."

"About kissing you. Which I don't regret one bit."

Jade cleared her throat, tugged at the neck of her button-down shirt. "Yes."

"She knows you were here last night and apparently, she's angry."

Their eyes locked and he wondered if she was remembering last night the way he was. A romantic dinner for two, candlelight, kisses that tasted sweeter than the ice cream she hadn't stayed around to enjoy.

A night that started so well and ended so badly.

A night when he'd told her he was falling in love. The big L word. L-O-V-E.

And she'd made appropriate noises that she might feel the same.

But somewhere the whole conversation had gone south and never returned.

"Which means she's watching your house, maybe following you."

Sawyer slapped both fists on his hips and growled low in his throat. "I hate this."

"You haven't touched anything, have you?" Jade jotted notes into her little notebook and snapped photos. "Leroy might be able to get some prints."

"We've been vandalized so often in the last two years, I know the drill. I've touched nothing except that light switch by the door and the refrigerator handle."

"Why the fridge?"

"I don't like hot milk."

The hint of a smile whispered against her lips. "Is the rest of the house like the living room?"

"This is the worst, but she paid my bedroom a visit. Might as well have a look."

Though reluctant and embarrassed to let Jade see what the demented vandal had done, he led the way to his bedroom.

Once inside, she drew in a long breath and let it out slowly. "Very personal."

"Tell me about it."

Rose petals covered his bed and a single red

rose lay limp, twisted and broken on his pillow. Someone, not him, had turned back the blue duvet, and the sheets were rumpled. Had someone been sleeping in his bed?

Jade emitted a small gasp. "Is that the rose…?"

Their gazes bumped before she turned her attention back to the bed.

"From your plate last night? That I bought for you?" If he sounded miffed, so be it. This morning, he'd tossed the rose in the trash in a fit of self-pity. "Yes, it is. She crushed it."

"Unrequited love is a powerful motivator. Someone you've rejected wants your attention very badly."

"None of this makes sense."

"Stalkers often don't. Their thinking is twisted." Jade snapped a couple more photos before heading back down the stairs, talking as she went. "I've been doing research on the mentality of stalkers, trying to get inside this person's head."

"Scary place to be."

"You're more right than you know." She stopped in the dining room and glanced at the table, now devoid of last night's romantic dinner.

"Want to sit in here and have a Coke while we wait for the police?"

She hesitated long enough to bother him before nodding. "You have any of that blackberry tea left?"

He smiled a little at that. The whole night hadn't been a failure. "Coming right up."

While he prepared the iced tea, she settled at the table with her camera and notebook in front of her. She scribbled something and then looked up at him.

"Your stalker is moving closer, getting more personal, angrier, more dangerous."

Invading his bedroom already reeked of crazy to him. He didn't want her any closer than that.

"Nice to know," he said wryly. "Thanks."

"I've been researching stalker profiles and their mentality. I'm seeing key characteristics here. You need to know what you're dealing with."

"Okay. Clue me in." He handed her the tea glass, popped a fizzy Coke for himself and leaned against the bar a few steps from the table to listen. "What I know about stalkers might cover a pinhead."

"Fortunately, most people never need to know." She flipped a page in her notebook as if looking for something. "Stalkers are obsessed with the object of their affections." She glanced up. "That would be you if, indeed, you were dealing with a stalker."

Grimly, he nodded. "Aren't I the fortunate one?"

"She wouldn't take no for an answer and she'd truly believe her victim loves her. Stalkers live in a fantasy world when it comes to the other person."

"You mean this woman thinks if she keeps this up, we'll be together?" That was seriously sick.

"Exactly. She doesn't see this as harmful to you. She thinks she's proving her love and if she hangs on, you'll come around."

Coke burned as Sawyer took a swallow. "Hard to do when she conceals her identity."

"In her fantasy, you know who she is and you love her."

"That's crazy."

"Probably. The profiles say she's delusional, a loner with low self-esteem and someone with few relationships, which makes her all the more desperate to have you, the object of her desire. And she's smart, smarter than average. Any of that ring a bell? Conjure up a name?"

"Not even a little ding."

"You need to tell your family about today's incident. All of them. I can talk to them, if you'd prefer."

"I'd rather Mom didn't know. She'll worry."

"Stalkers are nothing to mess around with, Sawyer."

Hair stood up on the back of his neck. "Are you saying she might hurt my family?"

Chapter Fourteen

Jade saw the fear in Sawyer's eyes, not for himself but for his loved ones. He looked as fierce and protective as a SWAT team.

No wonder she was falling in love with him. A man like Sawyer would not let his people down. Not when it mattered.

"She might, but for the most part and for now, you, not your family, are her focus. As long as she believes she has a chance with you, you'll remain the person on her radar."

The corner of his mouth lifted, though he was anything but amused. "Tick her off again and we can't predict what she'll do. Is that it?"

"Actually, I have a good notion of what the stalker might do, and it scares me, Sawyer." Scared her deeply. Sawyer could be in danger. A lot of danger.

Enraged stalkers had been known to murder their victims.

An awful thought suddenly slammed into her brain and prickled the hair on her arms. The stalker could be watching the house. She could know, right now, that Jade and Sawyer were alone together. At this very moment, some crazy woman could be plotting her next move.

Sawyer could be in danger because of his feelings for Jade. Because he'd kissed her. Because he loved her.

The truth hit her so hard, her knees threatened to give way. Sawyer Buchanon loved her. He hadn't been playing at romance last night. He loved her.

If she cared—and she did—she should get out of his house and leave him alone. For more reasons than one.

She paced to the front window and peered out. "I wonder why the police haven't arrived?"

"They were working a car accident out on the bridge." Sawyer tossed his empty soda can into the trash can. "I told the dispatcher not to rush. The house isn't going anywhere. And I'm safe."

"You may not be."

He froze midmove. "You think she's still around? Just waiting?"

"I think she might know I'm here and that knowledge could be dangerous. You have to avoid any situation that might send her over the edge." She fought the quiver in her voice. Staying cool was hard when someone she cared for might be in jeopardy. "Please, Sawyer. Take this very seriously and be careful. I don't want—" she glanced to one side, words falling to a whisper "—anything to happen to you."

Sawyer's heart leaped. He heard what she didn't say. No matter what had spooked her last night, she cared for him.

He crossed the space between them in three seconds, gently took the notebook from her, placed it on the table and tugged her hands into his. He longed to hold her close and forget about this crazy stalker business.

"I don't like this, Jade. You could be in danger, too. That scares me more than anything."

She pulled her hands away. Her lips trembled the slightest bit. "I trained as a police officer. I can take care of myself."

Her usual bravado was not convincing.

"You shouldn't have to. This nasty business is my fault and I won't have you in harm's way because of me."

"All right then, we're in agreement."

"Good. You'll let me protect you."

"No."

"No?" He tilted his head, bewildered, frustrated. She could be so annoyingly self-reliant. "But you said we're in agreement."

"That we can't see each other."

"What? No! I didn't agree to that. I can't." She'd

admitted she had feelings for him, but now she didn't want to see him. What sense did that make? "I'd rather you take yourself off the case and go home to Paris. You'll be safer there anyway until this stalker business goes away."

She shook her head. "No. I'm too close to stop. And trust me when I say this 'stalker business,' as you call it, won't go away by itself. She probably knows I'm here right now, and we both know I'm the cause of today's furious attack. But you're the one she's after, not me. I'm perfectly safe."

He wanted to argue but couldn't. The stalker was smart, smart enough to know about the romantic dinner, smart enough to know Jade was more to him than a business acquaintance.

"So what do we do?"

"We avoid each other as much as possible, and we can never, ever be alone together again."

He let two beats pass while the words soaked in. "What exactly are you trying to say?"

"Sawyer, I care about you." She reached out and then seemed to change her mind and let her hand fall. "But that's not important."

"It's the only important thing in this conversation."

"No. This is business, an investigation. I'm getting paid by your family. If I allow my personal feelings to interfere—"

"They already have."

"That has to end here. Now. Today."

"Is that what you want?"

"That's what has to be. We'll work together until this case is resolved but in the meantime we have to be more…professional."

"Professional?" After he'd kissed her? After he'd thrown his heart at her feet? "I'm starting to empathize with my rejected stalker."

"That's not funny."

"You got that right. I don't feel like laughing at all. I want to be with you, Jade. I have feelings for you. Strong feelings. You can't ignore that."

Feelings. Such a mundane term for the tsunami of emotion filling him up from the inside out. But for now *feelings* was the safest term. At least to his heart.

"I know, and I—" At the very second he thought she might admit to feeling the same, Jade stopped, frustrating him all over again. "We can't let this go any further. Being apart is for the best."

"For who?" He was getting riled up. Mad. Ticked. Hurt.

"For all concerned." Jade picked up the notebook and held it between them like a shield. She straightened as tall as a small woman could, her usually full lips prim and tight as she spoke. "I don't think things between us can ever work out, Sawyer, on any level and for many reasons. We should end it now and move on."

"Because of this crazy stalker issue? You'd let some nut job come between us?"

"It's more than that."

"Then explain it to me. And be very clear, because I must be stupid." He banged a fist against his chest, directly over the throbbing ache. "Tell me you don't care for me. Tell me that, and I'll walk away and never bother you again."

She glanced down, voice barely a whisper. "I can't."

"Then what's the deal!" He slammed that same fist into his palm.

Jade flinched. Her gaze flew to his face, eyes widening, pupils dilating until the gray formed only a thin ring on the outer edges.

He'd scared her. For one fraction of a second, she'd thought he would raise his fist and hit her.

His eyes dropped shut. His pulse banged with regret.

Jesus, forgive me.

Softening his demeanor, Sawyer stepped close again, voice lowered to a hush. "This isn't about the stalker, is it? This is about your ex."

She had secrets in her eyes as she shook her head. "You are in danger, Sawyer. I won't be the cause of a tragedy."

"Okay. Granted, but you're holding something back."

She crossed her arms, shut him out. "I don't know what you mean."

"You're afraid to trust me. You're afraid I'll

turn into your ex. That I'll hurt you. I wouldn't. Not ever."

It killed him to know she'd been hurt so deeply, that because of her ex she'd lost her trust in men, had lost a baby. A baby that would have been a little girl with her blond beauty or a little boy with her strength. A baby he would have adored.

She looked vulnerable and alone, though she didn't have to be. Not with him. Didn't she get it? He'd take care of her. He'd make her happy. He'd be the man her ex wasn't.

Sawyer couldn't help himself. "I love you, Jade. I'll never hurt you. We can work this out."

Her mouth dropped open the slightest bit. Her chest heaved. Emotion swam in her usually cool gray eyes.

Sawyer opened his arms and waited, vulnerable, accepting. If she rejected him, he'd live. He wouldn't want to but he would. But he had to hold her this one last time.

Just when he thought she might turn and walk away, she moved forward and leaned her head against his chest. Simply leaned.

He wrapped his arms around her and sighed deeply.

Now they were getting somewhere.

Jade nearly crumbled as Sawyer held her like a child against his thudding heart. She shouldn't have capitulated, but the hurt on his face had nearly done her in. She loved being here, near him, listening to his life source thrum for her.

"I'm not afraid of you, Sawyer." Granted, she'd flashbacked to Cam raising his voice and then his fist. But only for a second.

She wasn't afraid *of* Sawyer. She was afraid *for* him.

"I never want you to be. I want—"

She couldn't let him say it. "You wouldn't. I know that. But there are other reasons."

She loved Sawyer Buchanon, but if she said the words that bubbled and danced in her throat, she'd be lost forever.

A thousand emotions rolled through her. Love. Longing. Fear.

"We can work this out, Jade. Whatever it is." The words rumbled in his chest and tickled her ear, his voice full of emotion she couldn't let him feel. "All you have to do is tell me. We'll face it together."

A thousand conflicting emotions swamped Jade. She loved him. He was a good man.

She wanted so badly to cling to him and pledge her love. But she was afraid for him, too.

They couldn't be together. Too many barriers stood between them, and would remain even when the stalker issue was resolved—if there was indeed a crazed stalker. Part of her believed it. Part of her didn't, and those were facts she couldn't share with Sawyer. If he knew everything, would he want her then?

Her brother Bo could have ransacked this house. He could have written the note. He could have dumped the rose petals as a smoke screen. Those were exactly the things their father would encourage, applaud. "An eye for an eye," he'd say. "They owe us an eye."

No matter what else happened, the issue of her family remained. Her family. His enemy.

"I wish… If things were different…" She squeezed her eyes tight as Sawyer's heart thudded faster against her ear. "But they're not."

"They will be once we find out who this stalker is. We must be getting close or she wouldn't have upped her game."

Jade raised her head and soaked in his beloved face. "No. Nothing will change, Sawyer. We're too different. We won't work."

"What are you talking about? We have tons in common. The outdoors, skiing, funny movies, kids. We both love kids."

The words seared her like a blowtorch. They were good together on so many levels. "Our families are worlds apart."

"I'm starting to think you're grasping for excuses, looking for a way to let me down easy." He bracketed her face with both hands, pleading with eyes so blue and wounded, she almost capitulated.

She couldn't. Wouldn't. Especially now when he was in danger.

"Nothing unfixable," he said. "I care for you. You care for me. We'll work out the rest as we go."

Jade backed away, watching as his arms fell to his sides. If she had any integrity at all, she'd end this now.

"There are things you don't know."

"They won't matter."

Frustrated not to be able to get through to him, she dropped her head back and groaned. "Yes, they will. They will!"

"Try me."

"You'll hate me."

But that was what she wanted. Right? If he hated what she'd done, the lies of omission, the truth of who she was, he'd let her walk away from any hope of a relationship...and he'd be safe.

She licked dry, dry lips and blurted, "You don't know me. Not really. My maiden name is Clifton."

She waited to see if the name jarred his memory.

"Is that supposed to mean anything to me?"

"Your family and mine are enemies."

He tilted his head, a scowl narrowing the space between his eyebrows. "What are you talking about?"

"Hugh Clifton is my father." When he still didn't react, she went on. She might as well lay it all out. He'd learn the truth sooner or later, especially if her family was involved in the break-ins. "Clifton Concrete. Four Buchanon Built homes had to be demolished. A lawsuit."

Behind the puzzled face, Sawyer's mind worked and she knew the moment the name computed. "You're—?"

"Yes."

And before the initial shock wore off, before he could spew all the horrible things she knew to be true about her father, she turned and walked out of his life.

Chapter Fifteen

Dawson burst through the town house door less than a minute after the police car pulled into Sawyer's drive and ten minutes after Jade's bewildering departure. Sawyer turned toward his brother, leaving the officer to his investigation. He knew nothing about dusting for fingerprints anyway.

"What's going o—" Dawson froze in the doorway as he surveyed the topsy-turvy living room. "Whoa."

"You can say that again." Sawyer held up a hand, noting the throbbing bruise on his thumb. Was it only this afternoon he'd whacked it with a hammer and left work early? "But don't."

"What happened?"

"Other than my house being burglarized and the woman of my dreams telling me to leave her alone—permanently—nothing at all." Sawyer didn't try to hide the sarcasm. "I'm having a great day. A great week." If it got any better, he'd skip the next one and move right on to another month.

Dawson ignored the obvious destruction of personal property and homed in on the real problem, the one bumping around inside Sawyer like a lone tennis shoe in a clothes dryer.

"You and Jade had a fight?"

"A fight? Not exactly." He pinched his temples with thumb and finger. "I'm not sure."

"Did someone bonk you on the head? You're not making sense."

Sawyer rubbed his chest. The ache got worse. "That's the problem. None of this makes sense. A demented stalker who thinks I'm in love with her. Jade bolting on me because of something I barely remember."

Equipment jiggled as the police officer stepped around them and headed for the stairs. Sawyer grimaced. Gabriel's Crossing was a small town. Everyone would know about the rose petals by nightfall. He'd better steer clear of the Buttered Biscuit for a few days.

Dawson followed his gaze. "What's up there?"

"Rose petals, all over my bed."

Dawson's forehead scrunched up. "I hope Jade put them there."

"She didn't."

"Weird." Dawson blew out a long gust, a look of sheer yuck on his face. "Way weird."

"Tell me about it." Sawyer dipped to one side

to holler up the stairs. "Hey, Jim. Can we start clean-up down here?"

A disembodied voice replied, "Go ahead. I've finished dusting for prints."

Dawson tipped an end table upright. "Don't change the subject. What happened between you and Jade?"

"I cooked her a romantic dinner." Shaking out a giant black trash bag, Sawyer placed it in the center of the room. Some love this stalker had for him. He was about to lose some valuables.

"You cooked and she bolted. What happened? She get indigestion? Food poisoning? She's hating on you for bad cooking?"

"Not funny. Everything went great. I told her I might love her, we talked, ate, laughed, and then she ran out on me. I thought it was nerves or something. Then today, things got worse. Way worse."

"Whoa. Halt. Hold the phone." Dawson stared at him over the top of a busted lamp. "Back way up. You told her you *might* love her."

"Yeah, something like that."

"Do you?"

Sawyer rubbed that ache again. "I would if she'd let me. Every time I get close, she pushes me away."

"Bad breath? Body odor?"

"Would you stop? This is serious."

"Sorry. You're right." Dawson eyed the lamp,

shrugged and placed it next to the trash bag. "Maybe she doesn't feel the same way about you."

Oh man, he loved that lamp!

"I think she does. She said she cared and that if things were different, blah, blah, blah. Then, as if it was the biggest problem in the universe, she went into this white-faced admission that her family and ours are some kind of enemies. Like Romeo and Juliet or something."

"Who is her family?"

"I barely remember. Must have happened when you and I were at college." He squatted next to the fireplace where a clock had shattered on the hearth. His clock, for crying out loud! "Apparently, her dad and our dad had issues at some point in the past."

"Nothing new there. Dad has issues on a regular basis. That's where Brady, Mom and Charity work the spin."

"This was more than that. I remember when Dad had to completely raze some finished homes for structural defects. The finger of blame pointed at the concrete company."

"Her father's concrete company."

"Right. Hugh Clifton."

"Don't remember him." Dawson pointed at the scattered clock parts. "That clock is a goner."

"I love this clock." With the glass face now shattered, Sawyer traced his finger on the scripture reference. John 15:5 had become his life verse after Mom sent the clock with him to college as a reminder to keep his eyes on Jesus and off the world. Every time he'd been tempted to get a little crazy—and college presented plenty of opportunities—he would look at that scripture.

"Yeah, me, too." Dawson clapped a sympathetic hand on his shoulder and then left the room, returning with a broom and dustpan.

They scooped the clock guts onto the tray, working in silence for a few beats.

"So, you're upset with Jade for not telling you about her father from the start?"

Sawyer paused, a dismantled candle in one hand. Was he? "Maybe a little. The part about her dad's business doesn't bother me that much, but I don't like that she held back on me. She should have been straight up with all of us before she became our investigator."

His brother took the candle and tossed it into the garbage bag. "Hugh Clifton has nothing to do with the vandalism or trashing your truck, so I don't see a conflict of interest."

"Maybe Jade thinks he's responsible. Otherwise, why would she be so freaked out?"

"Ask her."

He rubbed the back of his neck. "She's the one that left. Shouldn't I take her at her word? We're done. Over. Move on. Quit being a hardhead who can't comprehend that a woman doesn't want him."

"Is that what you want to do?"

Hadn't he asked Jade the same thing? "No. I can't even muster the energy to be mad. Not about her family issue. Not even about the way she high-tailed it out of here as if I'd developed a severe case of Ebola."

"Doesn't sound to me as if that's what she wants, either. I think she's running scared."

A watercolor painting that reminded him of Broken Bow Lake lay facedown on the floor. He picked it up, saw the frame was loosened but the painting intact and gently stood it against the couch. This was something he could fix.

He wished fixing Jade were as easy.

"Her ex abused her."

Dawson, broom in hand, paused. He didn't have to speak for Sawyer to know his opinion of a man who hit women.

"There you go then. You gotta show her how a Buchanon man loves."

"I thought I was doing that."

"She trusted the guy enough to marry him. Then he betrayed her with his fists." Dawson's eyebrows lifted as he blew out a gusty breath. "Understandable if she harbors a lot of hurt. She needs proof that you're different. More time, more tenderness, more roses and dinners."

"You think the family issue is a smoke screen for what's really bothering her?"

"The only way for you to find out is to talk to

her." The other twin waved a hand around the ransacked room. "I got this. Go ahead. Give her a call and ask to meet up and talk this thing out."

Dawson the peacemaker, the mediator, the wise twin. Maybe he had a point.

"Thanks." Energized and hopeful, Sawyer whipped out his cell and stepped into the kitchen.

The phone buzzed in his ear. He let it ring until voice mail kicked in. "Jade. It's Sawyer. We need to talk. Call me."

In his vivid imagination, Sawyer saw her staring at the phone, unwilling to answer. She was still upset. She didn't want to talk to him. Yet.

Dawson suggested time and patience. Okay. He could be patient.

Until tomorrow.

Jade dreamed about spiderwebs. They were everywhere. In her hair, on her arms and legs, sticky and confining.

Somehow she knew she was dreaming. If she could wake up, the spiderwebs would go away.

Deep in her subconscious, she struggled toward the surface, struggled to wake up. Fluttering her eyes, she strained toward the light. The spiderwebs grew tighter, more frustrating.

She tried to run, battling the tangled webs.

Cam was coming. He'd hurt her. She twisted, tried to scream, but she couldn't get away.

A dream. She was dreaming. *Wake up. Wake up!* She tossed her head back and forth.

Out of the darkness, Cam appeared. Fear froze Jade in place. Her legs wouldn't move. She couldn't run. He came at her, fists raised and the familiar expression of rage. She could hear him rambling, calling her a liar and a cheat. He was going to hurt her again. Kill her baby. Kill her.

She cringed, awaiting the blows, the crack of bone, the taste of blood.

And then his face morphed and Sawyer stood there, a knife in his chest. Blood ran down his Texas Tech T-shirt. He stepped toward her and suddenly the knife appeared in his hand.

By now, the white lacy spiderwebs encased her like a mummy. She was paralyzed.

Sawyer raised the knife and gently, tenderly began to cut away her strictures. The webs stuck to his hands and tried to enslave him, too, but he slashed away the bonds, refusing to stop.

"I've got you," he kept saying. "It's the Buchanon way. I've got you."

Dear, wonderful man.

"Sawyer," she whispered.

Someone screamed.

And Jade jerked her eyes open, fully awake. Her heart thundered. The dream dissipated like water vapor. She breathed a deep sigh of relief. It was a dream. Only a strange dream.

She tried to sit up but couldn't. As in the dream, she was frozen in place, immobilized.

What was wrong with her? Why couldn't she move?

She heard a sound. Mice? She braced for a rodent to race across the bed. Slowly, she turned her head, expecting beady rat eyes to look back.

But the bloodshot eyes staring at her were brown…and human.

Startled, Jade jerked and tried again to sit up.

The woman laughed, though the sound was anything but pleasant. "Stupid. Stupid. Stupid. You're not going anywhere."

The only body part Jade could move was her head. Something was very wrong. Something terrible had happened to her.

She glanced down. Her cover sheet was gone. Silver duct tape bound her wrists and bare ankles. Ropes stretched from one side of the bed to the other, crisscrossing her chest, her legs, her stomach like spiderwebs.

"Oh, no." The adrenaline burst hit her. She fought against the ropes. "Let me up. Who are you? What are you doing?"

But she was afraid she knew.

The woman leaned over her, eyes glittering and a six-inch buck knife in one hand. "You know who I am. You know what you did. I warned you. I warned you both."

Scared out of her mind, Jade catalogued the

woman's description. If she got out of here alive, she'd need to describe her attacker.

If she got out of here alive.

She forced herself to breathe slowly and focus.

The woman was average height and weight, dark brown hair yanked back in a ponytail and black-framed glasses. Oval-shaped, ordinary face. A short, slightly flared nose. Freckles on her arms. No scars. No tattoos. No piercings. Not even her ears. Her captor was the kind of woman Jade had passed on the street a hundred times without noticing much at all.

"I don't know what you mean," Jade said. "Why are you here? What do you want? I don't have much money but you can have it." She motioned toward the desk with her chin. "My backpack is over there. My wallet is inside."

"You trying to buy me off? Love can't be bought. He's worth everything." The woman's face became menacing. "A trick. You think you can give me money and I'll walk away? I've invested too much. Sawyer is mine, not yours." She leaned closer and spat a swear word in Jade's face. "You can't fool me."

"Right. You're right. Nobody can fool you." Jade's mind raced in tandem with her pulse. She could think of no way out other than negotiations. She had some training. She could try. "Let's talk about this."

"Talk, talk, talk. You think I want to talk to

you? You tried to take him from me. But I won't let that happen. We're getting married."

Keeping her voice friendly, Jade said, "Congratulations. I'm happy for you."

"No, you're not. I saw you." The woman sneered. "All snuggled up with my man. He gave you a rose. Just like on that TV show. You got the rose. Well, I got one, too. Now you're trying to ruin everything. You took my rose. He bought it for me. I watched him at the flower shop, and I was so happy. But I won't have it. I won't let you steal what's mine."

The woman rambled, her words jumbled and fragmented.

Something had tipped the balance. The woman was out of control.

Jade tried to control the blood pumping through her veins at a crazy speed. She needed to stay calm. She needed to think. She was trapped. Her only hope was to convince the woman they weren't enemies.

"What's your name?"

"Nora Tipton *Buchanon*." Nora tossed her pony tail and touched the tip of the knife to Jade's nose. "Remember that name. Sawyer is mine. Or he will be once you're out of the way."

The woman whipped around and began to pace the room, mumbling and muttering. "She has to go. It's all her fault. The wedding must go on. She stole the rose. Kill her. Get rid of her."

Fear was a live snake slithering up Jade's spine, wrapping around every nerve ending. She considered a scream for help, but Nora would plunge that knife through her chest before anyone responded. If anyone ever did.

She wished Bailey still lived in the motel. She'd hear the screams and investigate.

No, that was stupid. Bailey could get hurt. She was a kid. Bailey and Ashton were right where they needed to be, safe with the Buchanons.

Whatever happened here today depended solely on her training and wits.

She licked her lips, searching for the right words. Her throat was as dry as Sahara sand.

"Tell me about the wedding, Nora. Who's your maid of honor?"

Ignoring the question, Nora paced to the window, peeked out and then paced back to the bed, only to repeat the motion twice more. She seemed lost in her own world.

"I'm always there for him. He said so. He told me. 'You're something special, Nora.' That's what he said. I knew then. He loves me. Sawyer's the handsomest man in the world and so sweet."

Yes, he was, and Jade was a fool for running out on him.

She pretended ignorance. "You're in love with Sawyer Buchanon?"

Nora, halfway across the room, spun around

and screamed, "*He* loves *me*! We love each other. That makes you angry, doesn't it?"

Calm, Jade, cool and professional. "No, of course not. Why would it? I barely know him."

How did this woman know Sawyer? Had they dated? She didn't recall Nora's name on any list of friends or girlfriends anyone had given her.

Behind a pair of glasses, Nora's eyes bugged and her face distorted. "Don't try to trick me. You think you're so smart, but I'm smarter. I see what you're trying to do to Sawyer and me. You want to crash the wedding. You want to stand up and object."

Keep her talking—get on her side.

"I'm not in your way, Nora. You can have him. I barely know the man. He's a client. I'm only the private investigator hired to find you." Jade tried for a shaky smile. "But I never guessed you were involved. You've been too clever for me."

A smug look settled over the woman's face. She eased back a little and focused on the empty wall as if watching a movie screen. "I was, wasn't I? And too clever for those one-horse cops and the Buchanons to figure out that sweet and helpful Nora from the Building Supply could get inside all those houses without anyone ever knowing."

The Building Supply. Sawyer went there nearly every day. Was that why Nora had focused on him? He was outgoing, friendly and nice to everyone. Were his visits enough to make Nora spin a fantasy that Sawyer's business stops were romantic trysts?

"How did you do it? How did you get inside? You must have devised a brilliant plan to fool everyone the way you did."

Nora pondered for a moment and then turned the knife over and stared at it. She slid a finger and thumb down either side, all the way to the point. "I guess it doesn't matter now if you know."

The words chilled Jade's very marrow. Telling the whole truth didn't matter because Nora planned to kill her. She was as good as dead.

Her body began to quake with the knowledge. The bed shook. Sweat beaded on her face and back, under her bindings.

Help me, God. Sawyer says You're good. He says You love me. If Sawyer is right, calm my mind and show me what to do. Send help. Do something. I'm so scared.

"Tell me all about it," she managed to say. "I admire cleverness."

"I *was* clever, wasn't I? So very clever. No one suspected a thing." The shiny, sinister blade gleamed in the light. "He shouldn't have been with that Lisa girl. Not after all we'd been together. She was snotty to me, and because of her, Sawyer wouldn't talk to me. He didn't even notice me."

Nora's grip tightened around the knife. She glared down at Jade as if blaming her for Lisa's behavior.

Jade braced for the worst, praying. Praying that God would forgive her sins and take her to heaven. Praying that she wouldn't die in the next moment.

"That wasn't very nice," she managed through teeth that had begun to chatter. "I'm sorry that happened to you. Maybe it was a mistake, a misunderstanding."

Crazed eyes roamed the room, unable to settle. "I showed her. I showed him. They can't get away with treating me like trash." She laughed her ugly laugh. "I had fun wrecking those houses. No one suspected me at all."

Keep her talking. Let her brag. "How did you get inside?"

Nora's attention stopped on Jade, a flitting housefly glance. "Every time one of the Buchanons came to the Building Supply to have a key made, guess who made a copy?"

"You. I'm amazed. Impressed. You're brilliant, Nora. The Building Supply is fortunate to have someone of your talents."

"I've been there ten years and I know everyone and everything. I know when the Buchanon crews take a day off. I know who is working where. I read the invoices. I even learned to drive the machinery so I would be indispensable. It came in handy when I moved their Bobcat last year. Everyone in town talked about that for days."

"And the fire."

Nora's face pinched. "That was Abby's fault. I saw her in the café talking to Sawyer. Cozy. She hugged him."

"But she married Brady."

"Because Sawyer wouldn't have her. I saw to that. I burned her dream house down and she had to move in with Brady."

Abby had done no such thing, but Jade was not about to argue. The woman's mind twisted facts to suit her fantasy. She was truly insane. Dangerously insane.

"Once you're dead, Sawyer will need comfort. He'll come to me. We'll finally be man and wife. Bride and groom." Nora hummed the bridal chorus and swayed, a soft, bizarre smile curving her lips.

Think, Jade, think.

"Sawyer isn't interested in me, Nora. I'm only the private investigator his father hired." Sawyer's Nancy Drew. "Naturally, I've had to interview him, but that's all."

As if Jade's words penetrated her insanity, Nora faltered. She blinked, confused, uncertain.

Thank You, God.

Then Jade's cell phone began to ring. Nora spun toward the desk and grabbed the device.

Her shriek shot Jade's blood pressure through

the roof. "It's him. He's calling you. You lied. You lied!"

"No, no. Nora, listen to me. He's calling about the case. About his house being broken into. That's all. The call is not personal."

Hang up, Sawyer. Please don't leave another message.

The ringing stopped. A minute passed while Jade held her breath and prayed, and Nora stared down at the smartphone with hate.

A beep sounded.

Oh, no. No, no, no! Sawyer had left a message.

Nora moved closer to the bed, knife menacing as she pressed the voice mail icon. "What's your password?"

Jade considered making one up to delay the inevitable, but a lie would anger Nora more. "There isn't one."

Nora put the phone on speaker. Sawyer's voice came on.

"We have to talk, Jade. Whatever happened, we can work it out. Call me."

The demented stalker shrieked loud enough to drown out the cars on the outside street, drew back and, with all her might, threw the phone at Jade. "You have to die. You have to die!"

Chapter Sixteen

Sawyer's sleep was anything but restful. He'd prayed, wrestled with the fact that his house had been burglarized and some crazy woman was still running around loose, all while trying to figure out where he'd gone wrong with Jade.

Not a single resolution had come his way.

This morning, with his second Coke and a bowl of Cheerios in front of him, he propped his bare feet on the couch and considered repainting the living room sooner rather than later. He'd taken off from work to complete the clean-up and figure out if his television was salvageable, but a fresh coat of paint sounded like a positive start. Anything to help erase the nagging thought that some malicious maniac had rummaged through his things and left bizarre declarations of love on his walls. And was capable of striking again.

Now he understood the word *violated*.

He glanced at his cell phone. No return call

from Jade. When he'd phoned Allison at the office, Jade had not yet checked in the way she normally did.

She must really be upset with him.

Be that as it may, his brother was right. They were going to talk.

He tapped in her number. After another series of buzzes, he left a message. Again.

Frustrated, he loaded the television into his truck and dropped it off at the repair shop before stopping at the Building Supply to look at paint samples.

While he sifted through the colors, a sales clerk walked past. "Can I help you, Mr. Buchanon?"

He half expected to discover the ever-helpful Nora leaning over his shoulder.

"Oh, hi, Anna. I thought you were Nora. She always seems to be around when I come in."

"Nora's out sick today."

"Sorry to hear that. Tell her I asked about her." He peeled a card from among the many in his hand. The color reminded him of Jade's eyes. Five gallons should do the trick. "I like this. Can you mix a five for me, satin finish?"

"Sure. We'll need a few minutes."

She left with the color chip and Sawyer roamed the building, a man's paradise, especially when that man was a carpenter. Today his mind wasn't on saw blades and power tools. It wasn't even on the stalker.

He couldn't stop thinking about Jade. Some inner nudge told him to try once more to reach her.

Probably his wishful imagination, but maybe she was thinking about him or ready to talk and too proud to make the first move.

Pausing in the plumbing aisle, he whipped out his phone and stared at her name. After a few seconds, he slid the device back into his jeans pocket and went in search of his paint. He'd give her a little more time, maybe invite her out to lunch.

He stopped by the Buchanon Built warehouse, more than halfway hoping to find Jade there. He didn't, and even a phone call from the business phone to her cell went unanswered. Yeah, he'd asked his sister to make the call.

The inner nudge to make contact grew stronger. Was something wrong? Was Jade okay?

"Nobody's heard from her today?"

"Not yet." Allison thumbed absently through a stack of mail while they talked. "She may have driven out to one of the houses without stopping here first."

"That doesn't make sense. She's studied those thoroughly, and since I'm the only one getting visits from our vandal these days, I doubt our construction sites are the target anymore."

He didn't like using the word *stalker* in front of his sisters. Taking Jade's advice, he'd warned them, though, about what had happened at his house and made them promise to be extra diligent. If something happened to anyone in his family because of him… The thought didn't deserve completion.

Allison put a hand to her back and stretched. Her tummy got a little rounder every day. "I hope she's not sick all alone at the motel without anyone."

He couldn't fathom being alone in sickness. Family always showed up in droves. Mama and Allison with food. Jaylee with green tea or something equally as revolting. Charity with a humidifier and an armload of medicines. Even his brothers popped in to give him a hard time.

Jade had no one.

Not true. She has you.

If he was looking for an excuse to see her, he'd found one. "After I grab a few paint supplies from the back, I think I'll head over to the motel and make sure she's okay."

"Great idea." Allison's smile was knowing, but then he didn't exactly hide the fact that he had a thing for the pretty PI.

Feeling better than he had since he'd walked into his wreck of a living room, Sawyer grabbed some brushes and rollers, dumped them in the bed of his truck and headed to the River Roost and the rough side of town.

As he pulled off the street and onto the gravel

parking area, he spotted Jade's white Chevy in front of her unit, next to an old brown pickup.

She was still at the motel? This late in the morning? And not answering her calls?

Yep. She must be under the weather.

He stepped out of his truck and gazed around the run-down area. Intense summer sun beamed on the dingy, shaded windows and the River Roost seemed quiet and peaceful. Nighttime was a different matter, and the reason he worried about Jade staying here alone.

As he approached the unit, he thought he heard a voice, but when he knocked the sound went silent. He waited. No one answered.

The TV maybe?

Mouth pressed into a firm line, he knocked harder. "Jade? I know you're in there. Your car's here. Are you sick?"

All remained quiet while he listened and the sun baked the back of his head. He raised his hand to knock again.

Before he could, Jade's voice permeated the wall. "Go away, Sawyer."

He leaned in, cupped both hands around his mouth and yelled, "Not until we talk. Not until I know you're okay. Are you sick?"

"No. I'm okay. Go away."

Her voice sounded funny. "Open the door. Let me see for myself, and then if you still want me to leave, I'll go."

"Please, Sawyer, listen. Leave. I don't want you here. We can *conduct business* later." Her tone was especially adamant. "I can't talk now."

Business? She knew he wasn't here on business.

An eerie awareness crept over him, prickled the hair on his arms. His gut screamed a warning.

He whipped around and scanned the area. Nothing. No one.

"Open the door, Jade."

Her reply was a frantic plea. "Go away! You have to leave."

Something was definitely wrong. "Open up now or I'll get the manager to let me in."

From the interior he perceived movement, a shuffling of footsteps. The lock clicked and the knob slowly turned.

He put on his best smile. "Now we're getting somewhere."

The door opened. A woman appeared. A familiar brunette woman who didn't look a thing like Jade. "We certainly are."

He blinked, bewildered. "Nora? Where's Jade? What—"

Sawyer's brain tried to make sense out of what he was seeing, but the next few seconds jumbled together like a junk drawer. He heard Jade cry, "Run, Sawyer! Run!"

But the warning came too late. Nora caught Sawyer off guard, grabbed his arm and yanked.

He stumbled into the room and fell to his knees as Nora slammed and relocked the door.

"What's going on in here?" He started to get up. Nora moved between him and Jade. The handy helper from the Building Supply held a knife the size of Florida.

Sawyer froze.

The fog of bewilderment dissipated. Sheer terror took over.

Jade tied on the bed. Nora holding a knife.

And he was on his knees, helpless.

If God be for you, who can be against you?

He wasn't alone. He wasn't helpless.

Sawyer drew in a slow, calming breath and prayed with all his mind for wisdom. And courage.

Slowly, he raised his hands above his head and played dumb. "Will someone fill me in? I'm kind of lost."

Very lost. But smart enough to know he and Jade were in deep trouble.

The saleswoman frowned. "You know what you did. I listened to her voice mail." Her face crumbled. "You're cheating again, Sawyer. After all we've been to each other. Over and over I've forgiven you. You're weak. You can't help yourself. These women won't leave you alone." She spun toward Jade and then back to him. "Like her. She seduced you. She's the reason."

Sawyer's heart stuck in his throat. Nora was his stalker? *Nora?* Pleasant, helpful, overeager Nora?

Cautiously, he rose to his feet, hands high, careful not to set the woman off.

He flicked a glance toward the bed.

"Jade," he murmured softly. "Are you hurt?"

"No." She held his gaze with particular intensity. "Nora has somehow gotten the wrong idea about you and me. I've been trying to explain that we are only business acquaintances. We are not romantically involved. Tell her, Sawyer."

"Is that true? Is she lying?" Nora stepped closer to Sawyer. He smelled sweat mixed with a sickly sweet perfume. Behind the glasses, her pupils had dilated to their fullest, obliterating her irises. Black, empty holes. "You can't keep cheating. I love you too much. I have to settle this once and for all."

Was the woman on drugs?

"Tell her, Sawyer. She needs to hear from you that she's the one, not me."

Aware of the message Jade was trying to send, he softened his tone and focused all his attention on his stalker. Nora thought Jade was a threat to her romantic fantasy. Convincing her otherwise was up to him.

What he did and said in the next moments could save Jade's life.

Lord, forgive the lies I'm about to tell.

"Absolutely true, Nora." He reached a hand toward her, cajoling, sweet-talking. If he'd ever had an ounce of persuasive charm, he needed to use it now. "Miss Warren is a private investigator hired by my father. I didn't want her around in the first place." That much was true. He hadn't wanted *anyone* on the job. "I thought hiring her was a waste of money."

"I want to believe you." Nora waved the knife in a circle. "You've hurt me so many times. All those women. You have to choose between these sleazy girls and me. You love *me*, Sawyer. I'm the one. The only one. I can make you happy." She pointed the gleaming blade toward Jade. "Not her. Never her!"

Sawyer watched Nora's every erratic movement, gauging, thinking. If he could catch her off guard, if he could go for the knife…

Nora might be crazy but she was smart. Angling her body to keep an eye on Sawyer, she stormed toward the bed and pressed the knife against Jade's jugular.

In a deep, guttural voice, she demanded, "Never, ever her. Do you hear me, Sawyer?"

Fear knocked against his knees. He nodded, afraid to look away from the woman, away from Jade's throat. If she moved that knife the slightest bit, he'd take action. He'd have no choice.

"Tell Nora how you feel, Sawyer," Jade urged, face white with terror. "Tell her she's the only one. She's concerned about the wedding."

Wedding? With him?

He swallowed, understanding what he had to do. Jade was in mortal danger. So was he unless they could convince Nora that she, not Jade, was the object of his affection.

"Nora, listen to me. Listen, sweetheart." He held both arms out to his sides, forcing a relaxed and pleasant stance. His heart was knocking through his shirt. "You're my special girl. I'm your man. Remember? You don't need to be jealous over Jade. She's nothing to me."

The words hurt but he had to say them.

Slowly, Nora lifted the knife from Jade's throat and turned to face him. Her lips quivered. "You gave her a rose. You cooked her dinner. Candles. I saw the candles."

The chill in his soul branched out until he felt cold all over. Had she watched them through his window?

"The rose was for you, sweetheart. I was only showing it to her. To be sure a woman as special as you would like it. I'm a guy. What do I know about flowers?"

"Really?" Nora blinked in rapid bursts. "You did that for me?"

"Absolutely. You're my special girl. Only you. No one else." He opened his arms, vulnerable, welcoming and cunning. "Come here. Let me hold you. I'm sorry if you misunderstood. I never meant to hurt you."

Nora's eyes widened and something shifted in the crazed depths as she looked with longing at the waiting embrace. Her chest rose and fell, her breathing loud in the room.

"You still love me?" A silver tear sparkled on her bottom lashes. "Truly?"

Now he was getting somewhere. She was softening.

"Let me show you how much." He tapped his chest. "Come to Sawyer, darlin'. I need to hold you, to feel your heart beat against mine."

If he hadn't been so scared, he'd have rolled his eyes. Never in his life had he ever made such a cornball statement.

Slowly, as if mesmerized by the prize before her, Nora edged toward Sawyer, away from Jade. The knife hand relaxed, fell to half-mast.

Blood roared against Sawyer's temples with enough force to take down a building. He had a plan. He prayed it would work. If it didn't, he and Jade were both dead.

He kept his focus on Nora and the knife, but in his peripheral vision, he saw the intensity with which Jade watched the scene being played out while she remained helpless. Once Nora's back was turned, she strained against the ropes, wiggling to get free.

He dared not look. Not yet. Not until Nora was in his embrace. He held the woman's gaze, willing her to come to him.

"I love you, Sawyer. You've made me the happiest woman in the world." A smile, rivaling the Joker's, spread her lips.

She walked into his chest and with a moaning sigh, wrapped her arms around his waist. He could feel the knife hand fisted against his back.

Nora raised her face to his. "Kiss me, my darling. Seal our love at last."

The idea revolted him. He wasn't sure he could.

Jade's life depended on it.

He'd never been much of an actor, but he closed his eyes, thought of Jade, and kissed Nora. She moaned again, kissed him long and hard, and then she buried her face in his neck. "Wonderful. Oh, Sawyer. My darling. At last."

Slowly, keeping her close, Sawyer released the hug and rubbed his hands over her upper arms. She tensed but he kept his stroke light and romantic, caressing her skin, gazing as tenderly as he could into her manic eyes.

After a few seconds, she shivered and raised her hands to his chest. The knife pointed inward, toward his thundering heart.

What do I do now?

The wedding. She wanted a wedding.

"Let's talk about our wedding." Get her talking. Keep her talking. Gain her trust. "We have plans to make. Should I rent a tux? Do you have your dress?"

She nodded, her face going dreamy. "Oh, yes.

I ordered it online. A lacy gown like Duchess Kate's. I saved forever to buy exactly the right one."

"You'll be beautiful in it." Along with the prison orange. "I can't wait for that day."

Carefully, he bracketed her face with both hands and tipped his forehead against hers. "All this time, I thought I was out of your league. Now here you are. Mine at last."

The words seemed to work. Like chocolate in the Texas sun, she softened, melting into him, relaxing. She believed him.

He would only have a few seconds while his body blocked her view of the knife. He had to move fast.

Adrenaline jacked into his bloodstream. His blood pressure spiked.

He kissed her forehead, and one by one her eyelids. As if hypnotized, her eyes remained shut. She moaned softly.

Now!

In a move he'd learned from wrestling his brothers, Sawyer spun away, grabbed Nora's wrist and twisted.

Her scream shocked his eardrums. She went wild. Incredibly strong for an average woman, she kicked and fought like a mad mule.

They tumbled against the bed, slammed into the nightstand. A lamp thudded to the carpet.

He felt a stick, a sting, and vaguely heard Jade's shout but couldn't make out the words.

Nora heaved against him, raising her knee. He dodged, threw her off balance and finally wrestled her down and sat on her back with his full weight of nearly two hundred pounds.

Repeatedly, he slammed her wrist against the carpet until she released the weapon. She bucked and raged, calling him every vile name. Threatening to kill him. To kill Jade. To kill his whole family.

Sawyer grit his teeth. *That* was never going to happen.

He shoved the weapon out of reach, yanked Nora's arms behind her back and looked around for something to tie her. If he could get to his shoelace or his belt… Better yet, he needed Jade's ropes.

All were out of reach.

"Sawyer, the lamp cord. Hog-tie."

He flashed a grim smile at Jade. "Smart girl."

In seconds, Nora's ankles and wrists were bound, though her mouth never stopped. She spat, screamed and reviled in between bouts of declaring her obsessive, undying love.

That kind of love he could do without.

Sawyer untied Jade and quickly called 911. Then he did what he'd wanted to do for two days. He wrapped his arms around her. "You're shaking."

"That's you."

"Adrenaline rush."

"You weren't scared?"

"Out of my mind." He grimaced, thinking of the woman on the floor, screaming obscenities. Above the din, he said, "Make that terrified."

While he waited for his pulse to return to normal, he searched Jade for wounds, for blood or bruises. Her wrists were striated red and raw. He lifted them to his lips and pressed gentle kisses there.

"Sure you're okay?"

"Yes, but you're not." She touched her fingers to his shoulder. "You're bleeding."

Texas red blood formed a softball-size circle on his shirt.

"A scratch." He shrugged away her concern and tugged her close. He kissed her lips, her hair, the red place on her neck where the knife had pressed. Oh, that red place. It broke him in half.

Nora's screams grew louder. "Liar. Cheater. I hate you!"

Ignoring the insults, he breathed in Jade's living, breathing essence.

She was safe. Nora hadn't hurt her. Jade was unharmed.

Thank you, Father God.

"I'm okay, Sawyer. Really."

He pulled back and pressed his hand against his shoulder. "I'm getting blood on you."

Jade tugged away his hand and lifted his shirt-sleeve. "Sawyer." She hissed through her teeth when she saw the wound, and then went into the bathroom for tissues. "You need stitches."

"Pressure works." But he let her minister to the cut and murmur over him in tender tones.

On the floor far enough away from them to be rendered harmless, Nora sobbed. "Liar. Liar."

Over the noise, sirens wailed and drew near. Rapid response. One of the blessings of a small town.

Jade tugged his sleeve down to cover the wadded tissues. "Promise you'll have the paramedics take a look."

"Sure." Whatever. He'd had worse nicks. A carpenter and his power tools sometimes tangled. "Gotta direct the police inside." He pointed to Nora. "Watch her."

"Gladly." Jade stuck a foot on Nora's back and grinned as Sawyer unlocked the door and stepped out into the heat. Jade. His super woman.

Fifteen long minutes, many questions and a bandage later, Leroy and a burly officer hauled the sobbing, incoherent woman away. Sawyer was stunned to learn Nora was the single perpetrator of every Buchanon break-in, including Abby's house fire. The woman was smart, conniving… and mad as the Hatter.

As the police cars pulled away, Sawyer stepped back into the motel room. He and Jade were alone at last.

They were finally going to have that talk.

Chapter Seventeen

His black hair stood out in a dozen directions, his shirt was bloody and his face scratched.

To Jade, Sawyer had never looked more wonderful.

Her motel room, however, was a mess. The lamp damaged, the bed rumpled, ropes and duct tape scattered about, and drops of Sawyer's blood on the carpet next to a wad of tissues and bandage wrappers.

None of that mattered now. Nora was in custody, the truth of her crimes revealed. She and Sawyer were safe.

The door clicked shut behind him. He stood with one hand on the knob staring at her.

"You're the most beautiful sight I've ever seen," he said.

Her lips curved. "So are you. I—"

Lightning fast and with a groan that could only

be relief, he swooped in and kissed her, lingering again on her neck where the knife had pressed.

Touched but giggling at his vehemence, she tried to pull away. She'd been in intense situations before. He hadn't. Not this intense. "You're the one who got hurt."

He shook his head and murmured against her skin, sending her pulse into orbit. "I lost ten years of life when I saw that knife at your throat. I'm so thankful—"

"Me, too." She tugged his head up and held a hand on each side of his jaw. Dear, gorgeous, brave and wonderful man. "I prayed. A lot. I prayed and God heard me."

"Yeah?" Hope flared in his beloved sapphire gaze.

"God was with me. I felt Him." She gulped back a tear. "He gave me the right words to say to Nora. And He sent you."

"Somehow I knew you needed me." He tapped his chest. "Inside, I knew. It was as if God was urging me to come here. I couldn't get away from the nagging need to see you. Immediately."

"I finally understand what you've been trying to tell me. God is not angry, He's not mean. He's a good, good Father like you said." Humbled by the revelation, she touched two fingers to her heart. "I feel His love. I've never had that before."

He tugged her hands to his lips, kissing one finger at a time. "Do you feel mine, too?"

She swallowed, emotion bubbling up inside. "Yes, I do. So much, I want to cry. It's…incredible."

Still holding her hands, he guided her to the chair and knelt before her. Emotion bubbled in him, too. She could see it in his face and feel it through his trembling fingers.

"We need to have a serious talk. About us." For once, he didn't smile. "If you kick me to the curb this time, I'll get the message. But first we get everything out in the open."

"I'm not kicking you anywhere." She was thankful for his perseverance. If he'd given up on them, she'd be dead by now.

He turned her hands palms up and traced her lifeline. "Are you saying—?"

"I've been afraid of trusting anyone, Sawyer, particularly a man, and specifically one like you." He loved her. She wasn't afraid anymore.

"One like me? What does that mean?"

"Charming and smooth with women. Too good looking for words."

"Stop." He tilted back, grinning. "My head can only swell so much without an explosion."

"Don't be thrilled. Those were not traits I admired."

He faked a cute wince. "Ouch."

"Hear me out. It gets better." She patted his forearm. "You were different. Still charming and handsome, but you have something that surprised me. Character. Integrity. Kindness. I couldn't believe you were for real. I didn't know what to do with you."

He sat back on his heels, contemplating and, bless him, understanding. "So you kept waiting for the other shoe to drop. For me to turn into Frankenstein."

"Irrational, I know, but I needed to be in control. With you, I was losing control. I was afraid of letting anyone get that close again."

"Because of your ex?"

"Him. My father. The church I grew up in. They were all harsh and controlling. My mother is still under my father's thumb. His word is law, and believe me, his is a judgmental, angry law."

"So you expected all men to be like them?"

"And all Christians. After Cam, I never gave anyone a chance to get close enough to learn differently. Now, I understand how wrong that was." She'd been as judgmental as her father.

"I'm not your ex or your father or any other loser who dared hurt you. The Christians I know are good people, well-intentioned souls. Imperfect but trying to be like Jesus. And I promise here and now, no man is ever going to hurt you again. Not as long as I'm breathing."

"I believe you." Sawyer was one of the good guys. With all her soul, she believed that. Jade blinked back grateful, happy tears, loving this man with an intensity that made her tremble.

"Over and over, your actions have proven you to be the real deal. Then today, you stood up for me. You put yourself at risk to protect me."

"And I always will. I—"

She pressed her finger to his lips, silencing him. She knew what he was about to say. He loved her. But until he knew everything, she didn't deserve to hear those beautiful words.

"Don't say anything more until you hear me out. I have a confession. Okay?"

He kissed her fingertip and grinned. "As long as you aren't going to run out on me again."

"I won't, although you may want to run out on me."

His eyebrows dipped together in a vee. "Why?"

"My family."

"I don't care about the past or the lawsuit or any of that."

"That's not what I mean." She took a deep breath. "I haven't been completely open with you."

"Okay. I'm listening."

"I passed my brother's truck out on the bridge and feared my father had sent him. I thought they might be responsible for the vandalism."

"Seriously? You thought your family devised the break-ins and set fire to Abby's house?"

Nodding numbly, she caught her bottom lip between her teeth. She couldn't read Sawyer's expression, but he had every right to be upset.

"Why didn't you tell me about this? Or my dad?"

"They're my family, Sawyer. I couldn't point fingers at them unless I was positive."

He studied her for several long seconds while her heart pounded and her mouth went dry. Had she lost him?

"Family loyalty?"

"That sounds stupid coming from me. But as messed up as they are, they're still my kin and I love them."

"What would you have done if they'd been guilty?"

She wanted to leave no doubt of what she would have done. She and Sawyer didn't need that kind of suspicion hanging between them like toxic fumes.

"Let me show you something." Going to the desk, she flipped open the little laptop, scrolled to her email and opened a file marked confidential. "Read this."

He peered over her shoulder. "It's to your boss. Are you sure I should see this?"

"Yes."

Silent as stone, he read the email and then clicked each of the attachments.

"All the files, my suspicions and every piece of evidence is there, including my father's and my brothers' names, addresses, the sighting on the bridge, the lawsuit records and their ongoing hatred of any mention of the Buchanon name. Everything."

His head swiveled toward her. "You were turning the case over to your boss."

"Sending this to Dale held me accountable. If my family was guilty, I had to know first, but I also had to do the right thing. For the case. For me. For your family."

Sawyer straightened, a smile slowly moving from his lips to the crinkled corners of his eyes. "And for us?"

"If you can forgive the deception."

"If there is one thing a Buchanon understands and respects it's family loyalty. It's the Buchanon way." He took her hand, reeled her in. "And I'm a real forgiving guy."

She fell for his tender words, hook, line and sinker. The bait was too delicious to turn down. "There's something else you need to know."

One black eyebrow shot up. "More confessions?"

"Uh-huh. Just one." She fiddled with the front of his shirt. "And I think you'll like it."

For once, the chatty man had nothing to say. He simply waited. But his heart pounded beneath her fingers.

"Sawyer Buchanon, you take my breath away. You fill the empty place inside me. You showed me how to believe when I couldn't. And I can't imagine my life without you in it."

"Keep talking." His voice rumbled in his chest, deep and emotional. "I like this a lot."

"I love you, Sawyer." She tilted her face up to his, a breath away from his lips. "Want to find out where this love thing might take us?"

"Oh, darlin'," he said in his best Texas drawl. "I'm already there."

Epilogue

Five months later, Jade made the trip from Paris to Gabriel's Crossing to attend the marriage nuptials of Quinn Buchanon and nurse practitioner Gena Satterfield. Today wasn't her first nor would it be her last time making this trip. Between the two of them, she and Sawyer racked up more miles than a frequent flyer.

Things were progressing well in their relationship. Very well. As her faith deepened, so did her love for her Buchanon man and his for her.

She'd never imagined a Buchanon would hold her heart in the palm of his hand. But hold it he did, and ever so tenderly.

On this momentous occasion three weeks before Christmas, Sawyer was one of Quinn's groomsmen along with his other two brothers while their dad stood as best man. The handsome Buchanon men, in black tuxes, white shirts, red ties and sprigs of holly and pine as boutonnieres, had decorated the church front as much as the red bows, greenery, white lights and candles.

Jade had soaked up the beautiful, faith-filled ceremony that sealed two people into covenant marriage for all eternity.

Forever sounded good these days.

After the wedding, guests moved into the fellowship hall, gorgeously festooned in Christmas colors. Jade, along with Bailey, made the rounds tasting the finger foods and the hot chocolate bar, and now waited for Sawyer to join her following more wedding photos.

A pianist softly played while guests roamed the room and chatted. The wedding, while not elaborate, seemed perfect to her.

But then weddings touched a sentimental spot she normally kept hidden, and Jade battled misty eyes as she sat at a white covered table with the handful of Buchanons who weren't in the wedding party, some she was meeting for the first time.

Bailey sat to her right, feeding grapes to Ashton. She'd thrilled at serving as keeper of the guest book and looked young and lovely in a red tartan dress with black leggings.

Allison, so pregnant she required help to get out of a chair, sat across the table with Jake, her watchful, hovering cowboy to his wife's left.

"Didn't you love that moment when the pastor said for Quinn to kiss his bride?" Abby, with her brunette hair and dark eyes, looked pretty in a belted burgundy sheath.

Jade nodded. Everyone had laughed and *ahhed* when Quinn whipped out a sprig of mistletoe to hold above Gena's head as they kissed. "The perfect Christmas touch."

"But completely out of character for Quinn." Jaylee, the ultra-fit sister, sleek as a cat in green velvet, nibbled on a small skewer of fruit.

"Which added to the surprise. Gena has mellowed him." Allison shifted positions, one hand to her immense belly. A curious expression moved across her face.

Jake frowned and leaned toward her. "You okay, babe?"

She batted her eyelashes at him. "I would be if I had some more hot chocolate and a cookie."

The former bull rider was up and moving before she completed her request.

Allison followed him with an adoring gaze. "He's the best."

Jade loved watching them together. They were endearingly devoted.

A pair of strong hands suddenly gripped her shoulders. Before she could whip around with an elbow to the solar plexus, Sawyer's warm voice whispered against her ear. "Miss me?"

Smiling from the inside out, Jade placed her hands over his. "Immensely. Can you finally join us for good?"

"All done." He took the saved seat on her other side, picked a chocolate-covered strawberry from her plate and munched.

As they talked and ate, enjoying the piano music while the bride and groom received guests and stared at each other with sappy happiness, more Buchanons stopped at the table.

Brady, the tallest of the brothers, scooted a chair up beside his wife and kissed her cheek. "Where's our princess?"

"Talking to Alabama." She pointed toward a tawny-skinned woman, Gena's office nurse who looked stunning in her Christmas-red maid of honor gown. "Lila's recruiting her to make her famous rocky road brownies for your grand opening."

"Aw, my little publicist."

Brady was in full swing with his yearly Christmas home makeover. Along with the Buchanon brothers, a passel of volunteers worked long and hard to make someone's dreams come true. Little Lila was not to be left out.

"Thank goodness we don't have to worry about an arsonist burning down the project this year," Abby said.

"We can thank my girl over here for that." Sawyer pointed a canapé at Jade and then popped it into his mouth.

"I'm relieved the case is solved, and Nora is no longer a threat to any of you or your property."

Sawyer tapped the top of her hand. "Or to you."

Yes, there was that. Jade still shivered to think how close she'd come to being killed by the insanely obsessed woman.

Karen, busy greeting guests, overheard the conversation and leaned in. "Nora is a sad, sick soul. Completely broken."

"You wouldn't say that if she'd hurt Jade or me."

Karen gave him a look. "Sawyer."

"I know, Mom. Compassion. Mercy. Even for Nora. God and I are working on it." He rose and hugged his mother. "You and the women's ministry are doing a good thing."

"I still can't believe her own family refuses to see her. She needs to know *someone* cares."

Karen and her friends visited Nora each week at the psychiatric hospital, baked goodies, sent cards and prayed for her. Jade admired the woman's ability to forgive and to love the unlovely. Like Sawyer, Jade was working on the forgiveness thing. Both with Nora and with her own family, particularly her father.

With a final pat to Sawyer's shoulder, Karen swirled back into the crowd, and the group broke up to move about and celebrate the occasion with guests.

The piano player slipped into lively Christmas tunes. Jade soaked in the festive, loving atmosphere, happy to be beside Sawyer as they chatted and laughed.

She squeezed his arm and he smiled down at her.

Someday, she wanted a wedding like this. Not exactly like this, of course, but a celebration surrounded by loved ones.

"Hey, why the sad look?" Sawyer dipped down to look into her face.

"Did I look sad?"

"For a second. You okay?"

"I was thinking about how different your family is from mine."

"You worry about your mother."

She did, of course. Mama was a doormat. A battered wife who wouldn't complain. "She won't leave Daddy no matter how he treats her."

"But she did drive down to Paris with you to shop. That's progress."

Leave it to Sawyer to find the positive. "And we're praying together on the phone, something we've never done."

"Keep praying. You might be surprised at what God can do with your mom…and your dad. He's still in the people-fixing business."

"You're so awesome. No wonder I have a mountain-size crush on you."

"Yeah, well, Gena's getting ready to toss the bouquet. Get on over there and catch it."

"Is that a hint?"

"Catch that bouquet and find out."

"Ooh, mystery man." Laughing, Jade sauntered over to the gathering of single ladies, where she caught nothing but a sharp high heel on top of her foot.

Afterward, giggling with Bailey and Jaylee, she limped toward Sawyer and waited for the bride and groom to make their departure. Holding hands and laughing, Quinn and Gena ran the gauntlet of artificial snowflakes and wildly ringing jingle bells.

"My brother surprised us all," Sawyer said as they started back inside the church. "As reclusive as he was for so long, I figured he'd sneak off and get married without so much as a witness."

"Love changes people."

His tender look melted her. "I'll say. You hated me and now look at us."

"I can't believe you didn't hate me in return when you found out my maiden name."

"It's not the Buchanon way." He winked. "We're lovers not haters."

He'd been supportive, not angry or resentful. And when her father had said horrible things to her when he'd learned she was dating a Buchanon, Sawyer had been there, comforting, loving, in his Buchanon way.

She tiptoed up to kiss him and was really settling in well when a shout arose. They both whipped around.

Jade's police training jumped to the surface. "What's wrong?"

Jake Hamilton, his face white as paste, cleared a path. Allison waddled beside him.

"Don't let him panic, Sawyer." Allison gazed around the crowd. "Where's Mama?"

Jake spun around on his polished boots, clearly in the midst of a panic Allison didn't want him to have.

Sawyer put a hand on the other man's arm. "Hey, bud. Settle. What's up?"

"Allison's in labor!" The cowboy scooped his wife into his arms and took off in a trot. "We're having a baby!"

Later that night, Sawyer gazed at the tiny baby sleeping peacefully in the hospital nursery. The corridor was packed with Buchanons roaming in and out, up and down.

The new mom was doing great. The dad not so much. According to rumors, he'd turned a few shades of green during delivery and slithered down a wall, and now sat next to Allison's bed with an ice pack on the back of his neck.

The cowboy was going to make a terrific dad.

"She's beautiful, Sawyer." Jade gazed through the glass at the very small bit of humanity. "All pink and perfect."

"I hope Jake doesn't teach her to ride bulls."

They chuckled together, exhausted but full of wonder at this day's occurrences.

"First a wedding and now a baby, all in one day."

"God is good to us Buchanons." Sawyer slipped his arm around the woman beside him. Love flowed today like the mighty Red River, pulling them all into its tender current. His insides were the consistency of grits—roughed up but mushy. "Someday, not too far down the road, I want a baby like her. Or two or three or seven. Don't you?"

"I'd like to get married first."

He tilted his head downward. "Is that a proposal?"

She gave him a gentle poke in the ribs. "That's your job, mister."

"Will you say yes if I ask? You didn't catch the bouquet."

She laughed. "Ask and find out. I may not be superstitious."

He was confident of her answer, but she needed the words. Words he had, plenty of them, crowding his heart and spilling out his mouth.

"Cruel." He sighed dramatically. "But so smart and beautiful. How can a man resist a woman such as you?"

Not caring one bit that he was in a hospital and half the world could see and hear, Sawyer took his love by the shoulders, turned her in his direction and stared into her eyes with all the emotion bubbling in his chest.

"I love you." He'd said the words many times but even a million wouldn't be enough.

Her smile widened. "I love you, too."

"That's good. Real good." Still in his wedding clothes, though he'd shed the jacket, he went to one knee right there in the maternity ward with hard tile digging into his bones. "Love is a good start, but we both know it takes more, and I promise you those things. A lifetime of commitment and respect, of working together with God at the center of everything we do."

"You're going to make me cry." Tears glistened on her lashes.

"You're the woman I've prayed for, the one I've waited years to find, my other half. Marry me, Jade. Today, tomorrow, next year. Just say you'll marry me."

Her lips curved as a single tear slipped down her cheek. His icy Nancy Drew had thawed so beautifully.

"Yes," she whispered. "Forever yes."

Dawson's voice cut through the medicine-scented air. "Hey everybody, look! Sawyer's proposing to Jade."

The corridor erupted with noise and footsteps as his family surged around them. Cell phones snapped photos and captured video.

Sawyer dropped his head. "No privacy in this family."

Brady whacked him on the back. "You're in a public place, knothead. What did you expect?"

"Leave him alone, Brady. He's trying to be romantic." Dawson shaped a heart with his fingers and grinned. "Go ahead, brother. Do your thing."

And so Sawyer rose to a stand and pulled his new fiancée to him, tilting her lips to his to seal their promise. She sighed against his mouth, sending shivers of pleasure up his spine.

Applause erupted. Someone whooped. He vaguely heard a nurse admonish them to be quiet.

His mother and dad and sisters and brothers, all the people he loved most in the universe, were here as witnesses. And Jade was in his arms.

A wedding, a baby and a proposal all in one perfect day.

He dipped back in for another kiss, his heart full of love and thanks and praise. God was good. Life was blessed.

And that, he thought with a smile, was the way he wanted it. Now. Forever. Always. He and Jade together, the Buchanon way.

* * * * *

Dear Reader,

As I finish up the Buchanon series with Sawyer's story, I hope you've enjoyed our time together in Gabriel's Crossing, Texas. Like most families, the Buchanons have their share of troubles but their Christian faith and family loyalty hold them together.

I set the Buchanon series in what is known locally as Texoma or Texoma Land, the Red River border area where Oklahoma and Texas meet. Though many people think of these states as flat, dry plains, Texoma is a beautiful area of forests, lakes, mountains and friendly small towns. If you ever have a chance to visit Texoma in the autumn, the scenery will take your breath away and the warm people will leave you with a smile.

I love to hear from readers. Connect with me at my website www.lindagoodnight.com or on social media. Be sure to sign up for my newsletter so we can stay in touch!

Until my next books, be well and happy.

May God bless you,

Linda Goodnight

Get 2 Free Books,
Plus 2 Free Gifts—
just for trying the Reader Service!

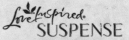

YES! Please send me 2 FREE Love Inspired® Suspense novels and my 2 FREE mystery gifts (gifts are worth about $10 retail). After receiving them, if I don't wish to receive any more books, I can return the shipping statement marked "cancel." If I don't cancel, I will receive 4 brand-new novels every month and be billed just $5.24 each for the regular-print edition or $5.74 each for the larger-print edition in the U.S., or $5.74 each for the regular-print edition or $6.24 each for the larger-print edition in Canada. That's a savings of at least 13% off the cover price. It's quite a bargain! Shipping and handling is just 50¢ per book in the U.S. and 75¢ per book in Canada.* I understand that accepting the 2 free books and gifts places me under no obligation to buy anything. I can always return a shipment and cancel at any time. Even if I never buy another book, the 2 free books and gifts are mine to keep forever.

Please check one: ☐ Love Inspired Suspense Regular-Print   ☐ Love Inspired Suspense Larger-Print
                         (153/353 IDN GLQE)   (107/307 IDN GLQF)

Name _____ (PLEASE PRINT) _____

Address _____ Apt. #

City _____ State/Prov. _____ Zip/Postal Code

Signature (if under 18, a parent or guardian must sign)

Mail to the **Reader Service:**
IN U.S.A.: P.O. Box 1867, Buffalo, NY 14240-1867
IN CANADA: P.O. Box 611, Fort Erie, Ontario L2A 9Z9

Want to try two free books from another series?
Call 1-800-873-8635 or visit www.ReaderService.com.

* Terms and prices subject to change without notice. Prices do not include applicable taxes. Sales tax applicable in N.Y. Canadian residents will be charged applicable taxes. Offer not valid in Quebec. This offer is limited to one order per household. Books received may not be as shown. Not valid for current subscribers to Love Inspired Suspense books. All orders subject to credit approval. Credit or debit balances in a customer's account(s) may be offset by any other outstanding balance owed by or to the customer. Please allow 4 to 6 weeks for delivery. Offer available while quantities last.

Your Privacy—The Reader Service is committed to protecting your privacy. Our Privacy Policy is available online at www.ReaderService.com or upon request from the Reader Service.

We make a portion of our mailing list available to reputable third parties that offer products we believe may interest you. If you prefer that we not exchange your name with third parties, or if you wish to clarify or modify your communication preferences, please visit us at www.ReaderService.com/consumerchoice or write to us at Reader Service Preference Service, P.O. Box 9062, Buffalo, NY 14240-9062. Include your complete name and address.

LIS17R

HOMETOWN HEARTS ♥

YES! Please send me **The Hometown Hearts Collection** in Larger Print. This collection begins with 3 FREE books and 2 FREE gifts in the first shipment. Along with my 3 free books, I'll also get the next 4 books from the Hometown Hearts Collection, in LARGER PRINT, which I may either return and owe nothing, or keep for the low price of $4.99 U.S./ $5.89 CDN each plus $2.99 for shipping and handling per shipment*. If I decide to continue, about once a month for 8 months I'll get 6 or 7 more books, but will only need to pay for 4. That means 2 or 3 books in every shipment will be FREE! If I decide to keep the entire collection, I'll have paid for only 32 books because 19 books are FREE! I understand that accepting the 3 free books and gifts places me under no obligation to buy anything. I can always return a shipment and cancel at any time. My free books and gifts are mine to keep no matter what I decide.

262 HCN 3432 462 HCN 3432

Name	(PLEASE PRINT)	
Address		Apt. #
City	State/Prov.	Zip/Postal Code

Signature (if under 18, a parent or guardian must sign)

Mail to the **Reader Service:**
IN U.S.A.: P.O. Box 1867, Buffalo, NY. 14240-1867
IN CANADA: P.O. Box 609, Fort Erie, Ontario L2A 5X3